Ashley
and the
Dollmaker

By

JARED JAMES GRANTHAM

A division of Squire Publishers, Inc.
4500 College Blvd.
Leawood, KS 66211
888-888-7696
www.leatherspublishing.com

To Ista Iola Taylor Grantham
The Dollmaker

ALSO BY THE AUTHOR

Ashley and the Mooncorn People

Contents

Prologue

$\mathcal{A}$SHLEY HOUCHIN had just completed a fantastic adventure in her own back yard in Prairie Village, Kansas. Just five days earlier this auburn-haired schoolgirl with the pixie smile had secretly rescued tiny Tork and Marie Dubois from a Mason jar buried beneath the stump of an old oak tree in her back yard. Willa Hauptman, a kind gypsy with extraordinary magic powers, had buried the couple there 100 years earlier to protect them. At the time, the now-dead tree was just a sapling. In the jar, Willa had also placed five magic mooncorn seeds, which Ashley had grown and the Duboises had eaten the night before, restoring them to their normal size. Willa had planned to bury Tork and Marie's children, Elie and Nicole, in another Mason jar beneath the next young oak tree she could find. Neither Tork nor Marie knew where the second tree was. It could have been anywhere between the Prairie Village site in which they were buried and Willa's ultimate destination of California, thousands of miles away.

Early in the morning following Tork and Marie's restoration, Ashley is awakened by the sound of a chain saw coming from her next-door neighbor Louie's back yard. She rushes to investigate and learns that Louie has just cut down a tree like the one her father worked on only a few days before. Louie asks Ashley to tell her father that he needs some help digging up the stump of the newly felled tree.

Louie's dead oak fills Ashley with hope. *Maybe Willa found that tree just a few steps away from the first,* Ashley thought. *I think Louie's tree was just as big as ours, so maybe Elie and Nicole and the other five mooncorn seeds are buried in a Mason jar under his tree!*

CHAPTER ONE

Mooncorn, so soon?

ASHLEY JUMPED UP and squealed ecstatically at Louie's request for her father to help him remove the stump from his yard.

"OKAY!" Ashley shouted as she rushed to her house next door.

Louie watched from his back yard, bewildered at Ashley's enthusiasm. *Gee, I wonder what she has against my dead tree,* he thought.

She flew through the back door, bursting with four days of grand adventures to tell her sleeping parents. But she stopped suddenly just outside their bedroom door as she was flooded with cautious thoughts.

Oh my! If I tell them that eating ears of corn caused tiny Tork and Marie to regain their normal size, I might not get the magic to work for Elie and Nicole. Besides, Momma and Dad might not even believe my story. I can hardly believe it myself.

In deep concentration, Ashley turned quietly and tip-toed into her room, slowly closing the door behind her.

Now what do I do? she thought. *I've got to think of a way to find the Mason jar under that tree before Dad*

1

and Louie hit it with a shovel. I don't want them to hurt Elie and Nicole.

Ashley lay on her bed, reliving the Dubois family's amazing adventures. Although their saga had begun more than 100 years earlier, Ashley had only learned of it a few days ago, when her father had brought down the dead oak tree and unearthed the Mason jar. Although her mother and father both knew of the jar, only Ashley knew its secrets.

Tork and Marie Dubois had been asleep in the jar for the past 100 years. A wicked gypsy named Ada Kohln had captured them from their farm in Belgium by giving them a potion that reduced them to only three inches tall. Ada kept them in a birdcage for her amusement. Willa Hauptman had rescued them from Ada and was traveling to California on foot when she fell terribly ill and had to revise her plan. Willa's magic was not strong enough to save her own life from the illness that had overtaken her, and she feared that she might die before the Dubois family was freed from the horrible spell that kept them tiny.

The secret to restoring the Dubois family lay in 10 magic corn seeds that Willa had to grow in the light of a full moon. Once the Duboises ate the corn, they would return to their normal size. The earth was dry from a long drought, and the next full moon was nearly a month away. She didn't think she would live that long, so she cast a sleep spell on the Dubois family and placed Tork and Marie in one Mason jar and Elie and Nicole in another. She divided the magic moon-corn seeds between the two jars and wrote notes to future rescuers alerting them to the tiny people inside.

Then she had to bury the jars under two young oak trees.

Unknown to Ashley, on the day Willa buried the first jar containing Tork and Marie, she was visited by a young girl carrying her rag doll and walking deep in the woods looking for berries. Willa was resting against a tree when the girl found her. The old gypsy appeared very ill, and the caring young girl ran to her and offered to take her to her home. Willa politely declined the girl's kind invitation, but she did ask her for a glass of water if the girl could bring it in secret. The girl, sensing that Willa was an unusual woman of great kindness and mystery, did more than that. She returned with cool water and a sack full of food.

She sat with Willa as the tired old gypsy ate for the first time in several days. While she slowly chewed, Willa told her young host about the Dubois family and the magic of the mooncorn seeds. Enchanted, the girl gently rocked her doll and listened at Willa's feet. After a couple hours Willa believed she had regained enough strength to continue her search for the second young oak tree. Before struggling to her feet to leave, the grateful Willa gave the little girl a long, tearful hug and an unusual gift that would change her life forever.

"Oh, phooey!" Ashley muttered. "Tork and Marie might have left Prairie Village by now. I hope they stayed close by. I've got a good chance to find Elie and Nicole, plant the mooncorn seeds and give them the corn so they can get big again like their parents."

She heard her parents talking in the hallway out-

3

side her room. When they headed into the kitchen she followed them and sat down at the breakfast table.

"Dad, I got up early to check on my plants and found that rabbits had eaten them," she said slowly, a mock look of sadness on her face as she fibbed about the mooncorn plants she had harvested the night before for Tork and Marie.

"Sorry to hear that, Ash. They were cute little corn plants. Well, at least I didn't mow them off or pick any more. Do you have any more seeds?"

"I think I know where I can find some, Dad," she said before chewing and swallowing a bite of cereal. "Oh, I almost forgot to tell you that Louie wants you to help him dig up a tree stump in his back yard, just like the one you did in our yard."

"Oh, rats," her father replied, pretending to be in pain. "That's not what I had in mind for the weekend. My muscles still hurt from that monster I dug up in our yard. But Louie is always helping me out, so I don't think there's a way to get out of this."

Later that morning, her father talked to Louie over the back fence and by afternoon both men were digging furiously around the stump of the felled tree. Ashley sat nearby working out a plan to find the Mason jar—which had to be buried among the tangled roots—before Louie and her father stumbled onto it.

By early evening, they had dug a hole several feet deep around the stump. "Louie, I've had enough for one day," Ashley's father said with fatigue in his voice.

"Me too, Jerry," Louie replied. "I should be able to finish the job by myself in the morning. Thanks a lot for your help. I'll treat you to a glass of iced tea on the

4

patio."

After the men left, Ashley jumped into the hole and crawled around the stump, looking and poking at the tangled roots and compacted dirt hiding Elie and Nicole. *Maybe I can dig around tonight and find the jar,* she thought.

CHAPTER TWO
Down Windsor Drive

THE NIGHT BEFORE, Tork and Marie had insisted that Ashley leave them alone to eat the ripe ears of the mooncorn plants. They took a few tentative bites, and then each devoured an ear. They sat quietly and smiled at each other, wondering what to expect next. In a flash of light so intense it temporarily blinded them, they were swept into a silent roiling cauldron of twisting and turning vapors that tugged at their arms and legs, stretching them longer and longer and longer. It ended as suddenly as it began. The night darkened once again as they stood naked in the moonlight looking at one another from adult height for the first time in 100 years.

"Are you okay, Marie?" Tork asked shakily.

"I think so," answered Marie, still trembling from the fantastic ordeal. "Let's get dressed and figure out what to do now."

A few blocks south on Windsor Drive, Iola was jolted from a deep, Kansas sleep by a surge of pounding energy rumbling through her body. Julie, who always slept beside her, was also awakened.

"Did you feel that?" Iola asked.

"Wow, did I!" Julie replied. "And I even saw a brilliant flash of light outside the window that must have come from the mooncorn house up the street."

"Well, Julie, I think we have our work cut out for us. Tork and Marie are now free to look for Elie and Nicole, and if I remember correctly, Willa was searching for another small, healthy oak tree to bury them under. I've wondered for nearly 100 years where that might have been. Willa disappeared, evidently heading west before I could ever see her again."

"Do you want me to go up there and check things out?" Julie asked.

"No," Iola replied. "I have a feeling that a very special little girl who moved in up there a few years back is deeply involved in this and has everything under control. We must be patient and let this take its own course. Never want to tinker with magic, right Julie?"

"Never tinker," Julie agreed, "but a little tweaking does help at times."

"Indeed, Julie. And you will have your chance to tweak before all is said and done. Tomorrow I've got to get busy and get this messy house cleaned up. Goodnight, Julie."

"Goodnight, Iola."

CHAPTER THREE
Back yard return

$\mathcal{L}$ATER THAT EVENING, after everyone in Ashley's and Louie's houses had gone to bed, she sneaked into the garage and found a small, clawed garden shovel, a crowbar and a flashlight. She decided not to use the silver shovel Tork had given to her just before he and Marie had eaten the mooncorn. She didn't want to damage it. She bent down and walked slowly to Louie's back yard and scooted into the gaping hole encircling the stump. She fell to her knees and shined the light on the roots and dirt beneath the stump. With the shovel and the crowbar, she dug and clawed the dirt away from the roots at about the same depth where her father had found the Mason jar in her yard.

Dig. Claw. Dig. Claw. Then she looked about, removing loose dirt with her bare hands. She used the flashlight sparingly, as the batteries were weak and the light was growing dim. The full moon had passed, and the hole was blacker than coal. She repeated the process over and over in the faint illumination of the Milky Way overhead.

She dug for about an hour, finding nothing. As she sat back in the hole to rest, she thought she saw some-

9

thing move on the top of the stump. She sat perfectly still and stared. Soon it moved again and then made a rustling sound followed by a loud flapping noise. Framed against the starry sky, it appeared enormous and eerily black. Ashley shivered in the warm night.

Maybe it's a vampire, she thought. *Or the wicked witch that lives down Windsor Drive.*

Ashley's cousin Lindsay had told her about the witch that lived in a spooky old house a few blocks south of Ashley's, and how she came out at night to scare little kids and eat them. One day Ashley had asked her mother about the witch on Windsor Drive.

"Oh, good grief, Ashley!" her mother exclaimed. "That old lady is no more a witch than I am."

At this moment, sitting in the hole and staring up at the phantom, Ashley wasn't so sure.

She fumbled in the dark for the flashlight, which she snapped on and aimed at the intruder above her. Two huge, orange eyes stared straight into her eyes, once again sending shivers thrashing up her spine.

"Whoo! Whoo!" the beast screeched, piercing the darkness with such force that Ashley's wildly beating heart jumped high in her throat. Suddenly, the creature flapped its giant wings and flew away into the night to find another little girl to frighten.

"An owl, it's just an owl," Ashley said aloud as she leaned back again, turned out the light and waited for her heart to slow to an imperceptible lub dub.

She trembled for several minutes, picked up the flashlight to look around Louie's yard for other creatures and then resumed her search for the Mooncorn Children.

After an hour, she rested again.

Maybe I got this all wrong. Doubt began to enter Ashley's thoughts. *Maybe Willa passed by this tree, and I won't find anything.*

But before defeat could overtake her mind, Ashley heard in the remarkable stillness of the night a clicking sound coming from a tangle of roots next to her face. There, she heard it again! Excited, but this time without fear, she shined the weakened flashlight beam on the area with one hand and dug with the garden tool in the other.

Click. Click. Click. The sounds grew more intense and seemed to be coming from behind one of the larger roots. She worked feverishly in that area, being careful not to poke too hard with the crowbar and risk breaking the jar.

She put the tool aside and removed the dirt with her bare hand, scratching and clawing deeper behind the root. And then she saw the magic words in the dim light: "Ball Mason." She wanted to shout and jump with joy, but she pursed her lips tightly instead as she removed the remaining dirt that had encased the jar.

Finally, she broke the captive jar loose from the earth and held it in her hands. The clicking had stopped and she could see no movement within, only a folded piece of paper. She grasped the jar lid with one hand and twisted, but her fingers slipped and the lid held fast. She clamped the jar tightly between her knees and with both hands gripped the lid so tightly her fingers hurt. She twisted with all the strength in her body.

The lid screeched and grated as it reluctantly let go of the jar it had sealed for 100 years. Ashley gently lifted the lid and aimed the flashlight into the open jar. She saw the folded piece of paper wiggle slightly as a boy giggled and then a girl. She gently removed the paper to find a tiny boy and girl with huge smiles on their faces looking directly up at her. They raised both of their arms directly over their heads in a triumphant pumping motion.

Ashley bent closer to the jar and asked, "Are you Nicole and Elie Dubois?"

"Yes! Yes!" they both cried out. "You have found us! Do you know where our mommy and daddy are?"

"I know that both of them are safe and are looking for you," Ashley replied. "They are as big as when you lived on your farm in Belgium."

"Hoorah, Hoorah!" came cheers from the jar.

"They are not here right now. I'll explain everything to you later. Right now I need to take you into the house and get you some water and food. By the way, my name is Ashley Houchin, and I found your parents just five days ago."

Ashley placed the jar on the outer rim of the pit, picked up the shovel and crowbar and replaced them in the garage. She returned to get Elie and Nicole and unfolded the note that was in the jar. She read aloud Willa Hauptman's request:

Please take care of my tiny friends.

"I will, I will," she said joyously as she gently hugged Elie and Nicole with her index finger.

Ashley took her new friends to the kitchen, removed some food from the refrigerator, drew a glass of water, walked slowly to her room and, juggling her bounty in her arms, eased the door shut. She laid the Mason jar on her bed so that Elie and Nicole could crawl out of their prison. Elie carried a lumpy sack containing the five remaining mooncorn seeds that were essential for their restoration to normal size. His shoulder-length, curly brown hair framed a handsome, rugged face. He wore baggy denim trousers and a long-sleeved shirt. Nicole had long, straight golden-blond hair that was in perfect harmony with her cover-girl face. She wore a pink cotton-print dress with puffed sleeves. They stood together on the bed smiling at Ashley, as cute a pair as she had ever seen.

Ashley knelt on the floor so that her face would be even with theirs.

"I am so excited to find you two. I helped your parents grow their mooncorn and harvest it. Everything worked just fine. And it will for you too."

She handed Nicole and Elie a thimble filled with water from which each in turn drank noisily.

"That tastes so good, Ashley. Thank you so much," Nicole said.

"Aye, Aye, Ashley," Elie chimed in.

As they drank and ate their first meal in a century, Ashley told them all she knew about their parents. How they spoke of their life in Belgium, the shrinking spell cast on them by the wicked gypsy Ada Kohln and their rescue by the kind gypsy Willa Hauptman. How they traveled with Willa throughout Europe, made their way to America and began a journey to California that was interrupted when Willa fell terribly ill and thought she was about to die.

"Elie, let's hope that the sound of the harmonica-flute you make with your fingers brings you and your parents together," Ashley said, reminding the children of the Duboises' plan to find each other once they broke free of the Mason jars.

"Harmonica-flute? Is that what you call this?" Elie asked as he put his thumb and index finger against pursed lips and blew between them with great force, creating an ear-shattering sound that rattled the cups and saucers in Ashley's tea set on top of her dresser.

"Sounds just like your dad's whistle I heard a few days ago. Wow, Elie!" Ashley exalted.

Ashley heard sounds coming from her parent's bedroom down the hall. She quickly threw Nicole, Elie and the Mason jar under the covers of her bed and covered herself up just as her mother opened the door and asked, "Ashley, was that you?"

Ashley slowly pulled the covers from her head and looked in the direction of her mother, who was framed in light coming from the hallway.

"Huh?" she asked dreamily.

"That strange sound that just about knocked your Dad and me out of our bed. That's what!"

"I didn't hear anything, Mom. Must have been Josh." At times Ashley liked having a mischievous younger brother to take the attention away from her.

"Are you up to something again?" her mother insisted. She hadn't forgotten Ashley's strange behavior over the last few days.

"Nope. Just trying to get some sleep."

"Okay. But no funny business."

"Nite, Mom," Ashley said as she sank back under the covers.

After the door shut, Ashley pulled the covers back to find Elie and Nicole lying face down on the other side of the bed.

"I hope I didn't hurt you, but I don't think we can let anyone know you are here or we might not be able to break the spell," Ashley explained.

"We're okay, Ashley. Just a little shaken up. It's been a big day for us."

Ashley picked them up, one at a time, and laid them in the same shoes their parents had slept in under her bed behind the bed skirt.

"We won't be able to plant the mooncorn for a month. But tomorrow we will look for your parents. If we are lucky, they might still be in the neighborhood. You two get a good night's sleep, and I'll see you in the morning."

They were asleep before Ashley could say good-night.

Sleep was much harder for Ashley to find. The excitement of rescuing Nicole and Elie and the challenge of locating Tork and Marie and raising another crop of mooncorn kept her awake until the first light of dawn oozed through the east window, where Tork had first signaled to her just a few nights earlier. But at last she came up with a plan and then drifted into a deep sleep.

CHAPTER FOUR

Homeless

D URING THE FOUR DAYS they were guests under
Ashley's bed, Tork and Marie had talked in detail about
the new things they had discovered in the 20th century.
Ashley had joyfully introduced them to automobiles,
paved roads, electricity, running water, indoor bath-
rooms and endless varieties of food and clothing.

Finding work would be a major problem since they
had no personal papers to show their identity. Ashley
had learned in Sunday school about the many homeless
people who wander the streets of America and how
they were able to survive because ordinary citizens were
not afraid to reach out to strangers. Tork and Marie
would be homeless as they crossed America searching
for Elie and Marie, so Ashley had suggested they stay
away from bustling downtowns and look for work in
residential areas. Older women and men work in their
yards a great deal and often need help. They might be
the Duboises' best source of temporary employment.
Most of the older residents would quickly judge that this
couple was not the criminal type. She suggested they
introduce themselves, explain they were homeless and
needed to earn money for food and shelter and were

eager to do odd jobs.

Now the time had come for Tork and Marie to put all of their new knowledge of modern America into action. The transformation from three inches to 5 1/2 -feet tall had left them both naked and breathless. Fortunately, the transition was painless. They had experienced only intense excitement and wonderment when, after more than 100 years, they viewed the world about them from an adult perspective. They put on the clothes Ashley had provided, a denim shirt and jeans for both, along with socks and shoes with laces. They took their first wobbly adult steps, taking care to avoid the gaping hole that had held them captive, and walked out the gate and onto the sidewalk of Windsor Drive. Their only possessions were the clothes they wore.

They walked a few blocks north to the center of a small park where they sat on a bench, partially hidden from the street by shrubs and trees. They looked all around, not speaking, while they gathered their thoughts and watched the first light of dawn peek through the canopy of branches overhead. When the sun had risen further and they could see people stirring about in their houses and yards, they set out in search of work.

They found many people tending gardens in the coolness of the summer morning, but unfortunately, after asking more than a dozen of them for work, they had come up empty-handed. They refused to get discouraged and walked on until they came upon an attractive woman with glistening silver hair kneeling as she pulled weeds in the garden beside her house.

"Hello," Tork said to the woman. "We are Tork and

Marie Dubois."

The woman turned her head toward them, sat back on her heels, smiled, took off the glove on her right hand and extended it to shake hands with both of them.

"Well, hello to you. I'm Betty Burns."

"This looks like pretty hard work, Betty," Tork began, "and we were wondering if you would want a helping hand."

Betty studied them for a moment, noting their kind faces. She rose to her feet with some effort and said, "Well, I suggest we get acquainted first. Come over here and sit down, and I'll get us some coffee. Have you had any breakfast?"

"No," Marie replied, "but anything you could spare would be most welcome."

Tork and Marie sat at a picnic table behind Betty's house. She returned shortly with muffins, butter, jam, fruit and a large insulated container full of coffee.

Tork and Marie did not know that Betty had been looking after down-and-out people most of her life, and she could spot them from afar. Betty saw something special in this pair. She could not put her finger on exactly what it was, but she was eager to find out who they were.

"Tork, is that right?" she asked as she poured his coffee. Tork nodded. "And Marie?" Another nod. "Where are you from?"

"Betty, we are homeless," Tork replied.

"Oh, I know that," Betty said, patting her thighs with her hands. "Tell me where you grew up and where you have been."

"Well, it's a pretty long story, and you probably

19

wouldn't believe it. But the short version is that we emigrated from Belgium, and we're trying to get to California to visit our children. They got separated from us weeks ago," Tork said, thinking that Elie and Nicole just might be in California by now. "A few days ago all of our clothes and money were taken, and now we have no papers to prove who we are."

This is one strange story, Betty thought to herself. *But I trust these two and would welcome some excitement in my life right now.*

"I'd say you have some very big problems, Tork," Betty replied. "But I've seen worse. Ever robbed or murdered anyone?"

"Huh?" Tork responded with a shocked look on his face.

Marie was more composed. "Betty, you don't need to be afraid of us. We've never caused anyone any trouble," she said with a voice so innocent and sweet that Betty knew immediately that, as she had suspected, these were very special people.

"I'll tell you what," Betty said. "I've got quite a bit to do around here. The garden needs a good weeding, I've got broken this and broken that all over the house, and my basement is a disaster area. Yes, I could use some help around here for a few days. I can't pay you anything, but I'll give you all you want to eat, and you can stay in my garage in a room we fixed up years ago for a boarder."

Tork looked at Marie and smiled, and Marie smiled back.

"You've got a deal, Betty," Tork said with a hint of excitement in his voice as he and Betty shook hands.

That should give us time to learn more about this coun-try and plan our search for Elie and Nicole, he thought.

CHAPTER FIVE

Searching for family

❧❧❧

ASHLEY WAS JOSTLED AWAKE by her mother shaking her vigorously by the shoulders.

"Wake up, Ashley! The morning is half gone."

Ashley rubbed her eyes with clenched fists that hid dirty fingers from her mother's view.

"Okay, Mom. I'll be up in a minute."

"Are you sure you didn't whistle or blow a horn of some type in the middle of the night?" her mother asked as she stood with arms akimbo. "Strangest sound I've ever heard, like a loud flute and harmonica duet, or something like that. Funny, though, it was strangely beautiful. I would have thought I was dreaming if your dad hadn't heard it too."

Her mother left the room, and Ashley jumped out of bed and pulled back the bed skirt. There they were, sitting in the shoe beds, smiling broadly.

"Elie, Nicole, are you okay?"

"We're great, Ashley," Elie replied.

"Today after breakfast I'm going for a ride on my bicycle, and I'm taking you along. We'll start looking for your parents."

Later, Ashley asked her mother if she could ride her

bicycle to a friend's house and play for a couple of hours.

"Mom, I'll need to make a detour to get there. I don't want to go by that spooky house down Windsor Drive. Lindsay insists that a witch lives there and that she eats little kids."

"Now I've told you before, Ashley, that is preposterous!" her mother retorted. "I go by that house every day of my life, and I have met the lady who lives there several times. I forget her name, but she's just a sweet, very old lady who has lived in that house for many years—long before either of us was born. I can't think of anyone more harmless."

"Just the same, Mom, I think I'll go around that house."

Ashley carefully put Elie and Nicole in a pocket and rode south on Windsor Drive. She was more than a little nervous, as she had never walked or ridden her bicycle more than two blocks away from home without an adult along.

She asked Elie to sound the signal as they rode slowly on the sidewalk. He blew away until it looked as if his eyes would burst. The piercing sound was loud, but not unpleasant. Ashley pedaled another block, and Elie made the sound again. She made a circuitous journey through her neighborhood that lasted about an hour. Curious people watched them ride by, but Tork and Marie did not appear.

Day after day Ashley and her little friends explored the streets all about her house, blasting out the mysterious sound that often startled joggers and walkers as they passed by. Ashley was beginning to get discouraged, and Elie's overworked cheeks looked more and more like balloons whenever he blew the signal.

Tork, Marie and Betty were getting very well-acquainted. One day just melted into the next as the homeless couple became Betty's close friends. Tork and Marie felt very much at ease and told Betty about their life on the farm in Belgium without mentioning the fact that it took place more than 100 years earlier. They spoke of Elie and Nicole and how they were eager to find them. But it was hard to know where to look. They could be around here, in California or anywhere in between. Betty told Tork and Marie how pleased she was to have their company.

These warm strangers helped to fill a deep emptiness in her life created when her husband, Earl, had to be placed in a nursing home. She wasn't concerned about their lack of identification papers or acquaintances, or the peculiar way they ended up in Prairie Village without their children. She would simply let events take her on a journey into the unknown.

When the few days they had initially intended to stay with Betty had passed, they gently explained that the time had come for them to move on. Betty was disappointed with the news and pleaded with them to stay longer, at least through the summer. She suggested that Tork could get a small job at a friend's gas station, no questions asked. There he could earn some money, so they could continue their search for their children more easily. Tork and Marie thoughtfully considered Betty's kind offer and eventually decided that they could use the additional time to explore the city in search of Elie and Nicole and save a little money as well. So Tork and Marie took up temporary residence with Betty, hoping all the time that Elie and Nicole might just wander by.

On a boiling hot summer afternoon in Kansas, Marie was watering flowers in the front yard as Ashley turned her bicycle onto Betty's street. Elie performed his signal on command, and the harmonica-flute sound reverberated through the neighborhood.

Marie was so startled by the sound that she dropped the watering pail on her foot. She had no time to feel the pain as she whirled around to face the street and immediately recognized Ashley riding toward Betty's house looking from side to side.

Ashley saw a woman running toward her. The woman stumbled and fell to the ground, got up, stumbled and fell again. Ashley suddenly recognized Marie and, throwing both of her arms in the air, crashed the bicycle into a wall of dense bushes that lined the sidewalk. Elie and Nicole tumbled out of her pocket and into the thicket.

"Ashley, it's you, it's you!" Marie yelled as she rose to her feet, tears streaming down her cheeks.

"Marie, it's me!" Ashley yelled back as she crawled out of the bushes to embrace her.

"Let me look at you," Ashley said. "You're taller than me! Can you believe it?"

"Do you have my children? I heard the signal."

"Yes, right here in my–" Ashley stopped in mid-sentence as her hand felt nothing.

"Oh, Marie, they must have fallen out when the bike wrecked."

Just then they heard children's voices coming from deep in the bushes. "Mommy! Ashley! We're okay. We're okay."

Ashley and Marie carefully separated the branches and spotted the children standing on the ground below. The soft leaves and branches had broken their fall, and except for a few scratches, they were unhurt.

Marie took a child in each hand and brought them lovingly to her cheeks, where they kissed her fiercely. No one spoke for a few minutes, as they hugged and kissed each other and wept for joy. After 100 years, the reunion was grand and sweet.

"I just can't believe it's you," Marie said to her children. "We owe Ashley and a nice lady named Betty more than we can ever pay." She turned to Ashley and kissed her forehead. "Thank you for everything, Ashley."

When the excitement had ebbed, Marie told Ashley that she and Tork were the guests of a wonderful lady who had found Tork a job. Betty was visiting her husband, Earl, at the nursing home, and she would not be back for several hours. Tork, on the other hand, would be coming home in a few minutes, so they could surprise him and have another grand reunion. With the experience of having lived secretly in Ashley's house, Marie thought that it would be easy to hide the children in Betty's home until the new crop of mooncorn plants was ready to harvest.

"Oh my, I've got to go!" Ashley exclaimed as she suddenly realized that she was due home soon. "I'll check in on you when I can. Give Tork a big hug for me." After kissing Marie, Elie and Nicole on the cheek, Ashley rode home to ready her special garden for a new crop of mooncorn.

The days passed quickly. Ashley saw her secret friends at times when Betty was visiting Earl. Marie stayed busy tending Betty's house, Tork worked long hours at the gas station, and Elie and Nicole watched television or listened to the radio from secret locations about the house.

At last, the moon turned full and Ashley planted the mooncorn seeds. This time the plants grew without any problems. On the day the plants became fully ripe, Ashley brought Elie and Nicole to her house to await the night of magic. And, indeed, the magic worked for Elie and Nicole just as it had for Tork and Marie. As before, Ashley was not present when Elie and Nicole were restored to their normal size, but this time she sneaked into the back yard shortly after they had put on their new clothing.

"Look at you!" Ashley exclaimed as she hugged them both, tears welling up in her eyes. "You're full size! But now I can't hold you in the palm of my hand."

Elie and Nicole stood facing Ashley with smiles stretching from ear to ear. Slowly they turned and embraced one another. Then, as the elder brother stepped away from his sister, he frowned, for he suddenly realized that he and his sister were exactly the same height. *This mooncorn magic needs a little extra work,* he thought.

A few blocks down Windsor Drive, Iola was awakened once again by a surge of energy within her body and the dazzling illumination of her bedroom and the forest surrounding her house. *The second jar was found, and now all four occupants are fully restored,* she thought with great satisfaction.

"Julie, you awake?" Iola asked.

"Yep, and I'm ready for some fun," Julie replied.

"It won't be long now, Julie. It won't be long now."

Ashley gave Nicole and Elie directions on how to get to the gas station where their father worked. They were to spend the rest of the night in the small park a few blocks away and then go to the gas station at sunrise, where their father would be waiting for them.

When Tork brought his children to Betty's that day, telling her that they had miraculously strolled into the gas station, the kind-hearted woman welcomed them into her home. No one ever knew if Betty believed any of this, but that didn't matter. For Betty had special magical gifts of judgment that served her well.

Ashley visited frequently at times when Betty was away, fearing that she might slip and say something about mooncorn seeds or other magical events. Neither she nor the Dubois family knew how far they could go in revealing the magic of the mooncorn seeds. Now was not the time to risk exposure.

The reunited Dubois family spent long hours telling about the adventures they had experienced over the last few weeks. And when that ground had been covered thoroughly, they began to reminisce about their former life in Spa, Belgium, which had changed so abruptly 100 years earlier. They wondered about their farm and the many relatives they had left behind to the point that homesickness fell heavily on them all. They had enjoyed Betty's hospitality and life in America, but they were compelled to return home, a force that Betty understood was irresistible. When they had acquired sufficient clothes and other necessities to strike out for their homeland, Betty organized a benefit at her church and raised enough money to purchase their airfare.

When the day for them to leave arrived, there were no easy ways to say goodbye. Only tears seemed to wash away the pain of impending separation. Betty regained her composure enough to insist that the Dubois family write often to her and come back for long visits whenever they could. Ashley met them in the small park near her home, where they exchanged hugs and kisses. She gave Elie and Nicole the Mason jar as a keepsake. They in turn gave her their tiny clothes to add to the silver shovel Tork had given her weeks before.

Ashley watched with the gifts held against her heart as the Dubois family drove slowly out of view up Windsor Drive, completing her adventure with the Mooncorn People.

Chapter Six
Windsor detour

THE REMAINING SUMMER DAYS passed quietly. Brother Josh and cousin Lindsay were good company and helped ease the sadness caused by losing close friends. Though younger than Ashley, they drew her into their play. She told them stories about little people and magic sunflower seeds, each time with a freshness of spirit and drama that left her young audience begging for more.

Eventually, Ashley began to think about the newly built school that she would enter that fall. As time for classes to start drew closer, she wondered how she would get to and from school, nearly a mile south of her home.

"Will I ride the bus to school this year?" she asked her mother, a hint of anxiety in her voice.

"No. You'll walk to school. It's a nice walk or bicycle ride down Windsor Drive. You'll have friends to walk with you."

Ashley looked dejectedly at the floor.

"Does going to the new school or having to walk worry you?" her mother asked, sensing some disappointment in her usually upbeat and adventuresome daughter.

"No, I suppose not. It's just that old spooky house down there that I try to avoid."

"Now Ashley, there's nothing to be afraid of. It's probably the safest place in Prairie Village. Look, I'll tell you what. Later today let's walk to school just for fun. We'll take Josh and Lindsay along. We can come back on Mission Road and get a Popsicle at the Food Mart."

Later that day the four adventurers marched off to school. All of the houses along Windsor Drive looked similar until they came to 79th Street, about three long blocks from Ashley's home. Along the entire east side of Windsor Drive between 79th and 80th streets ran a tall, black wrought-iron fence. Inside the fence stood huge trees surrounded by thick underbrush. About halfway along the block a gate marked the only entrance into this small suburban forest.

A narrow, winding path led from the gate through the dense trees to a white two-story Colonial house that was barely visible from the sidewalk.

"Mother, does the old lady you told me about live in that scary place?" Ashley asked as she, Josh and Lindsay peeked at the house from behind Mrs. Houchin's skirt.

"Yes, Ashley. I asked Louie about her just the other day, and he told me her name is Iola Taylor. She has lived there all of her life, about 100 years, I think."

"Dillon told me she's a witch!" Josh blurted out.

"Yes, Aidan says she's a hungry, wicked witch," Lindsay added.

"Now wait a minute, you guys," Mrs. Houchin cautioned. "I'm pretty sure she is not a witch, and she doesn't eat little kids on their way to school, or I would have heard something about it."

"Do I h-a-a-ave to g-g-go this way to sch-school?" Ashley stammered in a whisper. She wasn't so sure that Ada Kohln, the wicked gypsy who poisoned the Dubois family, or somebody worse had not caught up with her, the liberator of the Mooncorn People.

"It's the shortest way to school, honey. You can walk on the other side of the street if that will make you feel any better."

"Okay, I'll try it as long as the other kids are with me," Ashley replied timidly. She felt the hair on her neck bristle at the thought of walking by that spooky house twice each school day.

CHAPTER SEVEN

Windsor witch

CLASSES STARTED, and the walk to and from school became an important social event for Ashley and her classmates. They discussed school activities and important gossip every step of the way. Windsor Drive became a highway possessed by Ashley and her friends, a part of their lives as familiar as their own back yards.

For several weeks they walked on the west side of the street between 79th and 80th, looking intently across the street at the woods surrounding the old white house behind the tall iron fence. They never saw anyone come or go, and they never saw anyone in the yard or on the porch. Nor did they ever notice a door slightly ajar or any windows open to the breeze. Although the house appeared deserted and eerie, one day the children decided to walk bravely on the east side of the street.

They ventured that day, at a little faster pace than usual, along the east side. But everything went smoothly, so they tried it again the next day and the next day after that, and without realizing it the detour to the east side of the street became their routine path.

The children soon made up a verse to chant as they skipped by the old house on Windsor Drive:

Who's afraid of the wicked witch,
The wicked witch,
The wicked witch,
Who's afraid of the wicked witch,
The wicked witch of Windsor?

One day they gathered some fallen branches and dragged them along the iron bars as they skipped along chanting their verse. If they skipped at just the right speed, the wooden sticks hitting the iron bars beat in perfect rhythm with their chant, creating a tune they would sing for several blocks beyond the house. As they reached the end of the iron fence they would drop the sticks, letting them fall to the ground where they remained until the next wave of children skipped by.

October arrived and with it the first signs of fall. The leaves changed to yellow, amber, brown and crimson, and the fragrances of crisp breezes hinted of magical days ahead. One day on the way home from school Ashley and her friends walked up to the iron fence to pick up their sticks for the parade past the old lady's house, but the sticks were gone.

"I know we left them here this morning," Ashley said. They looked at each other and with a shrug walked slowly on, looking intently at the forest and the white house at the end of the narrow path.

Brendan stopped suddenly and yelled, "I saw something move in the window!"

"Where? Where?" Jessica asked.

They all stopped and stared at the nearly hidden windows.

Ashley was the first to speak. "Oh, you're just imagining things."

"Well, it sure looked like someone was there," Brendan said.

The children hustled home a little faster than usual.

"Mother, something funny happened today on the way home from school," Ashley said as she walked into the kitchen. "We march by that old lady's house every day and drag sticks on the iron fence. We never see anyone. But today our sticks were missing, and Brendan thought that he saw someone standing behind one of the windows."

"Well, Ashley, someone does live there. Iola Taylor, remember? She probably cleaned up her yard today and took your sticks."

"I just wish the lady would spend more time outside, so we could see her. I guess we'll think she's a witch until we can see for ourselves."

CHAPTER EIGHT

Witch gotcha!

SEVERAL DAYS LATER Ashley was heading home from school when she realized she had left a reading assignment in her desk. She told her friends to go on without her. She ran back to school, retrieved her book and once again headed for home.

Dark clouds circled overhead, and the smell of rain was heavy in the air. Ashley walked at first and then ran as fast as she could up Windsor Drive. The wind started to blow violently, and huge drops of rain mixed with hail fell from the sky in a torrent.

As she crossed 80th Street, she tripped over the curb and fell to the sidewalk on both knees. Pain ripped through both kneecaps, and when she struggled to her feet blood streamed down her legs onto her shoes. She fought back the urge to cry out as tears welled up in her eyes. She limped to the iron fence and pulled herself bar by bar through the storm past the overgrown property. Lightning cracked overhead, hitting one of the trees behind the fence. Splinters of wood spun through the air and crashed into the iron bars directly above her head.

Is the wicked witch trying to get even? Ashley asked

herself.

Lightning hit a telephone pole across the street, sending brilliant sparks flying up and down Windsor Drive. The lightning strike forced Ashley through the iron gate, and without thinking she ran to the porch for safety.

The front door of the house was open a few inches, but Ashley could not see inside. She stood on the porch trembling with cold and fear–fear not only of the storm but from being perilously close to the witch's lair!

Another thunderous lightning bolt illuminated the porch and the forest. Ashley turned quickly toward the door and saw a gnarled hand grasping its edge. The door opened farther. Knobby fingers reached toward Ashley, and a woman's soft voice spoke from the darkness just inside the house.

"Take my hand, dear. Come on in where it's dry and warm."

Jeepers, creepers! Ashley thought as she stood frozen on the porch in fear. *Something like this happened to Little Red Riding Hood and Snow White.*

The door opened more, and another bolt of lightning revealed a stooped lady about the same height as Ashley extending her left hand as she held onto the door with the other hand. A broad smile filled the woman's ancient face. She did not appear as Ashley had expected a witch to look, and the wet, cold little girl felt slightly more at ease.

"Come on in, dear. You're shivering and hurt. My house is warm and dry. We'll get you fixed up so that you can get on home to your mama." The woman spoke in a strong but pleasant voice that simply could not be that of a witch.

Ashley walked slowly into the front hall, and the woman closed the door behind them. Now they were surrounded by darkness, but the air was filled with the reassuring smell of potpourri. The woman struck a match and lit a candle that cast a magical glow on her, Ashley and the furniture in the front hall.

"There, now we can see each other and get acquainted," the old lady said. "The lightning strike put out my lights a few minutes ago. That was a dandy, wasn't it?"

Ashley nodded as she glanced nervously around the room.

"What is your name, dear?" the old woman asked.

"Ashley. Ashley Houchin. I live up Windsor Drive a few blocks. Thank you for letting me come in. I was scared stiff by the storm." *And by you,* Ashley added to herself.

"My name is Iola. Iola Taylor. I'll bet you've never heard that first name before."

"Yes, I have. My neighbor mentioned your name to my mother."

"Good. Good. Ashley, please come into my living room and sit with me until this storm passes. I'm sorry but I don't have a telephone, or we would call your mama. I'm sure she is quite worried about you."

Iola stepped slowly into the adjoining room and motioned Ashley to come along. The room was dark, except for the flickering candle and unpredictable flashes of lightning that revealed shelves lining all of the walls.

Another flash and Ashley saw what appeared to be

little children resting on the shelves. The shelves were filled with little children!

Ashley felt a strong urge to run for the door. Had the witch trapped her?

FLASH! Or were they dolls?

Iola raised the candle above her head so that it faintly illuminated the room. To Ashley's relief, she saw perched on the shelves dozens and dozens of dolls. The room was full of dolls. She was surrounded by them. Boy and girl dolls. Black, brown and white dolls. Their eyes sparkled in the pulsating light, creating a sense of movement and life.

"Oh my!" Ashley exclaimed, once again free of any fear. "They're, they're simply beautiful. And so many. Where in the world did you get them?"

"I made them all, with these two old hands. They're porcelain dolls," Iola replied as she showed Ashley her knobby, crooked fingers. "Are you comfortable, Ashley? Let me get you some dry clothes."

"Thanks. But I've really got to go. My mom will be worried sick about me. I'd better go on home."

"Well, here, take this towel and dry off. And clean up those messy knees if you can. You must have had a terrible fall. How brave you are, my dear."

As Ashley wiped off the blood, Iola continued. "Ashley, I've been watching you and your friends pass by my house for several weeks. You always seem so happy with your games and your singing. But I'm wondering why you think I'm a witch."

The question caught Ashley off guard, and she struggled to find the right words. "Well, your house is different from all of the others. It looks a little scary.

And we never see you in the yard. I guess we just decided someone who likes the dark must live there. A witch. Are you a witch?" Ashley asked bravely.

The lady chuckled. "Well, if I am, I'm a good one. I don't eat little children, if that's what you're worried about. Ashley, I've lived here for more than 100 years. I don't have any family nearby, and my eyes are weak. I have to avoid the sunlight, so I don't get out very often, and only at night.

"The other day when it was overcast I picked up your sticks by the fence. I secretly hoped you might come to the door looking for them. The storm brought you to me instead. You see, Ashley, I've been waiting for you to visit me for some time. I think we may know someone in common. Have you ever heard the name Willa Hauptman?"

"Willa Hauptman?" Ashley asked, her eyes opened wide. "Where did you hear about Willa Hauptman?"

Iola smiled, an impish look on her face. "Well, I met her once, a long time ago."

"My father dug up a jar this spring, and it had a note in it signed by a Willa Hauptman." Ashley's curiosity soared. "You say you knew her?"

"I'll tell you about it another day, Ashley. I want you to come back and visit me again. But you must come alone. There are some very special secrets about Willa that only you can know about right now. You have nothing to fear from a 106-year-old woman, but you do have a lot to learn."

"Could I hold one of your dolls before I go?" Ashley asked.

Iola reached over her head and pulled a beautiful

blond doll from a shelf and handed her to Ashley. Ashley studied the doll in the faint candlelight and stroked her long blond, lifelike hair. She pulled the doll to her chest and gave her a hug before handing her back to Iola.

"She's lovely. Just lovely. This is a day that I will remember forever, Iola. Thank you so much for helping me."

The rain had ended. A brilliant rainbow arched across the sky as Ashley left the house and ran up Windsor Drive to her home. She had completely forgotten about the nasty scratches on her knees.

CHAPTER NINE

Greetings from home

"MOM! MOM! You can't imagine what I've just seen! Wow!" Ashley yelled as she burst through her front door.

Her mother rushed from the kitchen, relieved to hear her daughter's voice. She had just hung up the telephone after calling Ashley's father at work to report their daughter missing.

"Oh, thank God you're home! I've been worried to death. Where have you been? Look at your knees, and you're wet as a sop!" Her words tumbled out.

"Mother, let me explain!" Ashley interrupted.

"Well, what is it? It had better be good!" Mrs. Houchin said with tears running from her eyes and hugging Ashley a little harder than Ashley would have liked.

Starting calmly, Ashley said, "I forgot my reading assignment and had to go back to school alone to get it. It started to rain. Then the lightning and thunder started, and I got caught in it as I was crossing the street next to the old lady's house. I tripped over the curb and skinned my knees. The wind was so strong that I was blown through the lady's iron gate, and before I knew it I was running to her front porch for cover."

45

By now Ashley was gesturing wildly, and her words were running together.

"Now settle down. Settle down," Ashley's mom tried to soothe her. "And try to give me a calm account of what happened."

"The door to the house was slightly open, and I could see this knobby old hand pulling it open. The old lady–Iola Taylor–asked me to come in to get out of the storm. Her lights had gone out, so she lit a candle so we could see each other. She's very old, over 100, I think she told me. Lived there all of her life. And you know what? She knew Willa Hauptman!"

"Who's Willa Hauptman?"

"Good grief, Mother! The name on the note in the jar Dad dug up."

"Of course, now I remember. Go on."

"Iola is very nice. She has been watching us since school started, and she was a little sad that we thought she was a witch. She said that if she was a witch she was a good one. Oh, Mom! You just can't imagine what's in that house! I saw one huge room filled with dolls of all kinds. She called them porcelain dolls. They had hair that looked real and beautiful eyes with lashes. They looked so lifelike."

"Did she tell you why she had so many dolls?"

"No, but she said that she would tell me about the dolls someday. She made them all herself. Oh yeah, I have to come alone. She promised me that she didn't eat little children. Can I go, Mother? Please?"

"Ashley, why don't you ask me again tomorrow? Right now I'm still a little flustered about your late arrival from school. Your dad's going to come storming in here pretty soon all upset because he could not find you. She's a sweet, harmless old lady, I know, but let's talk it over, okay?"

"Mom, I promise to play by your rules and won't stay longer than you tell me I can. I think that Iola has a lot she wants to tell me without others around. Please let me visit her one more time alone," Ashley begged.

Her mother paused for what seemed an eternity and then said, "I'll let you know tomorrow, and that is final."

"Okay, Mom." Ashley backed off as she sensed she was close to getting permission to visit Iola again.

"Now get cleaned up for dinner, and prepare to meet your father's fury."

CHAPTER TEN

Christmas dolls

THE 3:30 BELL RANG, and all the children headed for the doors. Ashley's mother had told her that morning that she could visit Iola for 30 minutes after school. Ashley met her friends and told them she had to stay late to work on a reading project. Five minutes later she headed for Windsor Drive and Iola's house.

It was sunny and bright, unlike the day before. She paused at the iron gate and then slowly walked to the door looking for signs of movement in the house. She knocked three times and took a couple of steps backward. In a few moments, she saw the doorknob turn slowly. The door opened, revealing the smiling lady she had met the day before.

"Hello, Ashley. I'm so glad you came back to see me. Won't you come in?"

"I'd like to visit today, but I promised Mother I would only stay for 30 minutes. Is that okay with you?"

"That's fine with me and your mother. She stopped by this afternoon, and we had a nice chat. I told her what a fine young lady you are and that I wanted you to stop by as often as you can."

"Did you show her the dolls?" Ashley asked.

"Indeed I did, and she was very complimentary. You must have done a pretty good job describing them to her. Come on. Let's go sit in the parlor with my friends."

They entered the magical room that was filled with beautiful dolls. A dazzling beam of sunlight streamed through the south windows, setting the room ablaze and illuminating the dolls with a magical glow. Ashley was overwhelmed with delight. She imagined that this must be what it is like in doll heaven. For a moment she thought she could hear the dolls chattering as some of them gazed at one another and others looked squarely at Ashley.

"Mrs. Taylor—"

"Call me Iola, dear," the old lady interrupted.

"Iola, I've been thinking all day about what you told me yesterday. You know, about Willa Hauptman. I never knew her, but she left notes in two jars she had buried under two trees near our house."

"Yes, I know, Ashley. Let's see if my memory is correct. The trees died last winter, and I'll bet your father dug up the first stump this spring. And you were in for a big surprise. Right?"

"Right on! Wow! How did you know that? But wait a minute. How did you know about the tree and the jar? And did you know about the Mooncorn People?"

"Mooncorn People. What an interesting way to put it," Iola responded. "Well, they were described to me as the Dubois family from Belgium. To their good fortune, you were the one who found them."

"They are my very special secret," Ashley said. "Willa had given them some seeds—mooncorn seeds—that I planted for them. Tork and Marie Dubois stayed under

50

my bed for several days while they waited for the ears to develop in the glow of the full moon. They ate the corn that grew on the plants and changed back into their normal size. The very next night after they left I found their children in another jar buried in the roots of another stump. Willa didn't have to go all the way to California after all. It took awhile to get the Dubois family put back together, but with the help of a kind lady everything worked out for them just fine. Now all four of them are back in Belgium."

"Ashley, that's just the way Willa would have wanted it to work out. How very wonderful you are, young lady."

Iola went to her chair and sat down, motioning to Ashley to sit on the floor at her feet. "Ashley, I met Willa Hauptman about 100 years ago. I was almost six years old, and I lived right here in this house. The nearest neighbors lived a mile away. Prairie Village was just a few houses clustered together on the other side of that big hill you live on. My father farmed this land and worked very hard from dawn to dusk just to put enough food on the table for himself, my mother and me. I was the only child.

"We had had a very dry spring. The crops were shriveled up, and we barely had enough hay to feed our cattle, horses and goats. One day I took a walk in the woods looking for wild berries up on the hill, near where you now live. To my surprise, I found a gypsy lady sitting on the ground, leaning against a tree. She looked very ill. Her cheeks were sunken in, and she had dark circles under her eyes. Her clothes were tattered and very dirty. I remember being a little frightened

51

of her at first, just like you were of me. Right, Ashley?"

"Right, Mrs. Ta—, Iola," Ashley replied sheepishly.

"The gypsy spoke to me in the softest, sweetest voice I'd ever heard. She asked me my name and then told me she was very ill and was going to die soon. She asked if I would get her a cool drink of water. I remember I raced home, filled a burlap-covered jug with cool well water, gathered some cookies, side meat and bread from the kitchen and ran back to her. I helped her drink the water and eat the food. She propped herself up a little higher and then she told me her name, Willa Hauptman. And she told me the story about the miniature Dubois family, the magic mooncorn seeds and how in 100 years the tiny people would be freed once again by a sweet princess. That princess was you, Ashley, wasn't it?"

Ashley nodded shyly.

"Willa felt a little better after she had eaten. I offered to take her to my house," Iola continued, "but she refused, saying she would lose all of her powers if she sat in the woods with more than one person who was not a gypsy. Then she asked me a most unusual question: 'What has been the greatest disappointment in your life, Iola?'

"The question caught me by surprise, but the answer came to me in a flash. I told her that on every Christmas Eve we went down the road to our church for a traditional service. A large pine tree in the church was decorated with brightly colored balls, tinsel and strings of popcorn. Each year at least 20 new store-bought dolls were placed under the tree to be given to the little girls in the congregation. They were always so beautiful. I'd never had a store-bought doll of my own, and the previous Christmas Eve I believed that one of those dolls would be for me.

"After an agonizing wait, the time came to hand out the dolls. One by one the names of the girls were called, and each walked to the front to get her new doll. I crossed my fingers and wrung my hands each time a girl walked back to her seat with a huge smile on her face and a new doll in her arms. It seemed to go on forever. Finally, the last doll was given out, and, as in the years before, my name had not been called. My heart was broken. My mother leaned over and gently whispered to me, 'Iola, I'm so sorry, but we couldn't afford to buy you a doll. Things are so very hard for us right now. Maybe next year.'

"I could feel the tears gush into my eyes and a thick lump rise in my throat. I put my head in my hands to hide my disappointment from the other children," Iola continued. "On the way home in the wagon that night, I pledged before God that if I ever had the money when I grew up, no little girl I knew would ever go without a doll at Christmas.

"When I told Willa my story, she turned to me with an unusual glint in her eyes and said, 'Iola, dear, I have just the thing for you.' And she pulled from the fourth finger of her right hand a golden ring with a large opal setting. She placed the ring in the palm of my left hand, grasped both of my hands in hers and chanted some words in a language I'd never heard before or since. I felt intense heat in the palm of my hand, and just when I thought I couldn't stand it anymore, Willa spread my fingers apart. The opal was ablaze with light that filled the dark woods about us. Soon the light faded to a faint glow, and the ring cooled. Willa told me to slip the ring on one of the fingers of my right hand and to never take it off.

"She told me that as long as I kept the ring, I would have the power to make beautiful dolls and to talk to them, and they to me. She told me that I could make as many of these doll friends as I wanted. And should I decide to give some of the dolls away, when their owners were finished with them they would find their way back to my house, and they would tell me everything they had seen and done."

"You mean that you can talk to these dolls?" Ashley asked in disbelief as she looked about the room.

"Yes, I can, dear. But, Ashley, neither you nor anyone else can hear what they say. I'm the only one with that power."

"Are you kidding me?" Ashley asked, unsure whether she should believe this lady's tale.

"No, dear. In fact, each of these dolls has a very interesting story to tell. Everyone in this room has returned to my home after staying with a little girl until she grew up. Perhaps if you decide to come back to visit me, I can tell you some of their stories."

"Do you really have a magic ring?" Ashley asked.

"See for yourself." Iola bent down and placed her right hand in Ashley's lap. On the first finger was a magnificent opal set in a golden ring. The stone had a faint glow, like an ember in a smoldering fire. Ashley noticed that Iola's hands were very knobby and deformed from arthritis, yet these were the hands of an artist who could make porcelain dolls that were lovely beyond belief.

Ashley stared intently at the ring for several moments, and then her eyes rose to meet Iola's friendly gaze. "I'll be back tomorrow," she said.

"Remember, Ashley, just like with the Mooncorn People, you cannot tell anyone about the magic of this ring until I say so, or the spell may be broken."

"Oh, I understand. See you tomorrow."

CHAPTER ELEVEN

Good wind, bad wind

ASHLEY REPORTED TO HER MOTHER on time and told her Iola's story about the Christmas dolls. But she left out any mention of Willa Hauptman or that Iola could talk to the dolls. It didn't take Ashley long to convince her mother that she could visit her new friend for a few minutes after school each day.

The next day school dragged on endlessly, but finally the 3:30 bell rang and Ashley raced to Iola's house five minutes behind the other children. Iola had left the front door ajar and was waiting inside for her.

"Hello. I'm here!" Ashley called through the gap in the door.

"Come into the parlor, Ashley," Iola replied.

Iola was sitting on the couch holding a doll with long brown hair, brown eyes, high cheekbones and a face graced by a broad smile.

"Ashley, I want you to meet this young lady. She is the first doll that I ever made. She is nearly 100 years old. You will learn her name later," Iola said.

"Hello," Ashley said as she reached to shake the doll's hand. The doll wore a long white batiste gown decorated with luxurious blue embroidery. She looked so lifelike that Ashley imagined that she heard the doll return her greeting.

"This story involves two young girls, about your age, Ashley," Iola said, as she arranged herself in her chair so that she could put the proper body language into her story. Ashley, still admiring the doll, sat on the floor and looked up as Iola began:

This doll's story began very near to where we are today. After I made her, I gave her to a little girl named Mary Louise Dunlap, who was visiting relatives here in Eastern Kansas at Christmastime. Her parents had had serious problems with their farming in Eastern Missouri, and they had come to Kansas to live with relatives until a new farm could be located. Mary Louise did not receive a doll at the annual Christmas celebration, so I gave her this one before the party had ended. You can't imagine how thrilled she was. And me too! Her parents finally found a new farm near Louisville, in the hills of Eastern Missouri, just a few miles from the Mississippi River.

The other girl, Carol, lived on a farm several miles north and east of Mary Louise, but the girls had never met. Carol was the youngest of four children, and her two brothers and sister regarded her as the baby of the family. They always looked out for her, but they were known to occasionally tease her and to refer to her as the baby.

Carol's father raised cattle and pigs and grew enough grain and hay to feed the livestock, which they sold at the market. They made just enough money to buy essential items to keep the family going. Carol's mother managed a tidy house and still had time to plant a huge garden that supplied canned vegetables and fruits for them to eat all year long. Money was very scarce. Carol only had hand-made toys and cloth dolls. She had never had a store-bought gift of any kind.

One summer afternoon storm clouds gathered in the southwest, and the sky turned an angry green color. It was tornado season, and Carol's family watched anxiously as the storm came closer to their farm and the wind began to blow violently. Her parents had called the children to the house to watch the gathering storm together and to look for the telltale funnel clouds that everyone feared.

"Look, just over the tree line to the southwest!" Jim, the oldest brother, yelled.

Indeed, coming fast out of the southwest was a boiling layer of greenish-black clouds that covered the sky. And just in front not a mile away, hanging lower down, was the funnel of a marauding tornado, voraciously consuming trees and buildings as it screamed toward Carol's house.

Her parents hurried the family into the storm cellar next to the house with little time to spare. The heavy door guarding the cellar was slammed closed behind them and latched tight. They huddled in the dark, musty cellar fighting cobwebs and spiders as the storm thrashed overhead. The cellar door rattled and banged, and the wooden beams overhead shook furiously, stirring up clouds of dust that drifted onto Carol and her family.

The noise intensified, and a powerful draft ripped the cellar door loose from the latch. The winds threatened to suck the family out of the cellar. Reacting quickly and with uncommon strength, Carol's father grabbed the door handle and held on tight. Still, the winds raged stronger, opening the door again and lifting his body off the ground. Jim raced to his father and grabbed his legs. Paul and Elinor then grabbed hold of Jim. Carol and her mother also latched on. Through the rest of the storm, the family clung to one another and kept the door safely shut.

After what seemed an eternity, the wind and noise subsided and this pile of frightened humans began to release their grips on whatever or whomever they had been holding onto. No one said a word. They simply looked at one another, grateful for the quiet but afraid to leave the safety of the cellar. Carol's father moved first. He slowly climbed the steps until he was high enough to open the cellar door. From the top step, he turned full circle to see the land and sky all around him and motioned for the rest of the family to join him.

They were greeted by bright sunshine and overjoyed to see that the tornado had passed through a large pasture just to the south of their house and barn, leaving the buildings unharmed. They walked together to inspect the damaged pasture. The usually knee-high grass was flattened and twisted, and debris was scattered as far as they could see. Broken tree limbs, bottles and shingles from other homes and barns several miles away were strewn about.

As Carol walked along the edge of the tornado's path, she was startled by the sight of a small pale leg protruding from a large clump of pasture grass.

Could it be the leg of a baby? she asked herself.

She was so frightened that she didn't dare look any further. Instead she screamed for help:

"Momma! Daddy! Jim! Paul! Elinor! Come quickly! Please!"

Her father arrived first.

"Daddy, I think there's a baby in that clump of grass."

Her father studied the area and then bent down and gently lifted out a beautiful porcelain doll with long brown hair, brown eyes, high cheekbones and a broad smile. He straightened the doll's clothing. With a broad smile on his face, he handed the doll to Carol and said, "Here, Carol. The doll you've always wanted just dropped in."

Carol cradled the doll in her arms and examined it lovingly. There was not a scratch or a blemish on the porcelain parts, although the dress was torn and smudged with dirt. Carol instantly fell in love with the doll and without wondering where it had come from or whom it might belong to said, "I'll call her Julie."

The family spent the rest of the day rounding up the live-stock and accounting for all of the farm buildings and equipment. Later in the evening, Carol made a bed for Julie next to her own. After a brief conversation with her new friend, Carol fell into a deep but restless sleep.

In a dream, she saw herself carrying Julie through the woods near her house into a large field covered with golden daffodils. In the distance, Carol could see a house with several horse-drawn wagons and carriages parked about. People were standing on the porch dressed in their Sunday best. Sad gospel music came from within the house. She walked quickly to a side window and standing on tiptoes looked into the large front room. Some people were sitting in chairs, and others were standing around the edges of the room. Everyone was looking toward a wooden box on top of a pedestal. In the box lay a young girl about Carol's age.

She seemed to be asleep. Some people were crying; others were singing a mournful song about "Crossing the Bar." Then a man dressed in a long black robe read from a book as more people in the room began to cry. The little girl in the box did not seem to notice any of this. She lay perfectly still.

Soon everyone in the room rose to their feet and walked out to the front porch. Carol went up to a young woman who had walked to the edge of the porch and asked, "Why is everyone here?"

The young woman said, "This is a funeral for Mary Louise Dunlap, who was killed yesterday by the tornado."

Carol took a step backward, holding Julie more tightly to her chest. She had never seen a dead person before. The thought of someone her own age dying took her breath away.

"Young lady," the woman asked, "where did you get your doll? Mary Louise had one just like it that was carried away by the tornado. She tried to run after the doll and was hit by a large flying tree branch. Where did you get that doll?" she asked again, sounding a bit hysterical.

Carol jumped back in fear. Then she turned and ran toward the field of daffodils. Two large German shepherd dogs saw her escaping and chased after her, barking loudly. Carol ran as fast as she could for the safety of the woods and her own house, the dogs nipping at her heels. Monsters leered from the woods, and barnyard roosters flew around her head pecking at her ears.

Suddenly Carol bolted straight up in her bed. "Momma! Momma! Help me! Help me!" she screamed.

Her mother rushed into her room and folded Carol into her arms, saying, "It's just a dream, dear. It's just a dream."

Tears flowed down Carol's cheeks. "Oh, Momma, it was awful!" she sobbed. "That poor little girl. And Julie. I stole Julie from her, and now she's dead."

"It was just a bad dream, dear, just a bad dream. Easy now," Mother soothed Carol as she put Julie into bed with her daughter. "We'll talk about it tomorrow. Now go back to sleep."

Carol's mother sat on the side of the bed until Carol had drifted to sleep. She could have sworn that she saw a twinkle in Julie's eye.

In the morning her mother consoled Carol until she was settled enough to talk about the terrible dream. Carol told the story in great detail. She also admitted that before her dream she never even considered that her beautiful new doll might have come to her through another girl's suffering and loss.

Carol and her mother decided that they should retrace the path of the tornado to find Julie's owner. By late afternoon, Carol's father had outfitted a horse and carriage, and she and her mother drove onto a trail that followed the general direction of the oncoming tornado. They passed through the pasture into a thick forest that nearly covered the bumpy trail, which had been cleared of fallen trees and other debris earlier in the day.

After several miles, they came to a field of golden clover that had been trampled by the tornado. At the far side of the field, just on the outskirts of Louisville, they saw a farmhouse with a broad front porch.

"Momma," Carol said breathlessly, "it's the house I saw in my dream. But the yellow flowers are clover, not daffodils like my dream." Carol looked about warily for the raging dogs and monsters that had chased her the night before.

Her mother drove steadily toward the house. A large, black wreath hung on the front door, indicating someone in the family had passed away. No one was around. She stopped the horse and stepped out of the carriage to tie the reins to a hitching post.

"Come along, Carol, and bring Julie with you," she instructed her daughter.

Carol and her mother walked to the front door, and her mother knocked on it. In a few moments a woman dressed in black opened the door slowly. She recoiled when she saw the small girl holding the porcelain doll.

"Oh, my God! Oh, God!" she cried as she put her head in her hands. "Where did you find Mary Louise's doll?"

Carol's mother calmly explained, "We've come from the northeast looking for the owner of this little doll. We found it in our pasture after the tornado passed by yesterday afternoon. We would have come sooner, but we've had a lot to do at our farm to get things put back together."

The woman began to sob loudly and then fell to her knees in front of Carol and Julie. Carol gently placed a hand on the woman's head, and the grieving mother reached up and clasped their hands together.

"I'm sorry to act like this, but this doll belonged to my Mary Louise. It was blown away from her by the storm. My daughter was killed as she tried to rescue her doll."

"Yes, I know," Carol said bravely. "I saw it all happen in my dream last night."

Carol's mother explained to the woman how her daughter had found the doll and later in a dream had seen the dead girl at the funeral in this very house.

"My goodness, yes. We had the funeral here earlier this afternoon. How remarkable."

"We had intended to give the doll to its owner," Carol's mother said. "But we can pray that it will bring you some comforting memories of Mary Louise. Oh my, the sun is setting, and we must return home before darkness falls

64

in the forest."

After Mrs. Dunlap and her mother had embraced, Carol, with tears streaming from both eyes, gave the doll a final hug, kissed her forehead and slowly handed Julie to Mary Louise's mother.

They made the lonely trip back home as darkness fell across the trail. They were not bothered by any dogs, monsters or flying roosters along the way.

The next morning Carol awoke, sat up in bed and looked at the empty doll bed beside her. The painful disappointment of the day before returned, and in the early morning light she slowly sank back onto her pillow and cried softly. *Perhaps someday I will have another doll as beautiful as Julie,* she thought. In the meantime, she would be brave and grateful for the brief time that she had shared with her special friend.

Just as the tears stopped, Carol's mother opened her door and asked, "Carol, are you awake?"

"Yes, Momma."

"Well, dear, if you go to the front porch, you will find a pleasant surprise."

Carol jumped out of bed, rushed through the house and threw open the front door. On the porch, bathed in brilliant rays of the early morning sun, was Julie, propped against a post that supported the porch roof. Carol raced to the doll, pulled it tightly to her chest and pirouetted across the porch to inaudible music of joy. After she turned several dizzying circles, her mother caught the small whirling dervish and pressed her and the doll to her apron.

"Oh, Momma. You bought me a doll just like Julie! Oh, thank you, thank you, thank you!"

"I'm glad you like the doll, Carol, but there is more to it than that. This morning I found her right here on the porch with this note pinned to her dress." Carol's mom pulled a piece of paper from her apron pocket. "Mrs. Dunlap must have left her here early this morning. Let me read the note to you."

Dearest Carol,
 Mary Louise loved this little doll more than life itself.
I think she would be pleased to know that her precious
friend was loved by another little girl just as much.
You may give the doll any name you wish, but I think
you might want to know Mary Louise called her Julie.

Iola paused for several moments as she watched the tears welling up in Ashley's beautiful eyes. She gently folded Ashley's hands in hers and said, "Now Ashley, there is much more to learn from our friends in this room. Come back another day, and I'll tell you of Twadie's travels."

CHAPTER TWELVE
What is black?

ĬT WAS DIFFICULT for Ashley to keep these amazing secrets to herself. Her classmates began to question her about the after-school activities that kept her from walking home with them. Several times she almost blurted out about the magical house where Iola Taylor spun her tales. On one occasion when the subject of the spooky house on Windsor Drive came up, Ashley interjected, "I've heard that a nice old lady lives there and that she isn't a witch at all. She's just very old and can't see very well in the daylight."

"Ashley, you always look at things from the bright side," Jessica snapped. "I still think she's a witch."

"Think what you want," Ashley said, "but I'm not going to sing the witch song anymore. If she's not a witch, it might hurt her feelings."

From that day on, none of the children sang the wicked witch song as they skipped by the iron fence in front of the white house on Windsor Drive.

At the end of the next school day, Ashley made up a new excuse for staying late and then hurried to Iola's house, where she found the front door slightly open in anticipation of her arrival. Ashley let herself in and announced, "I'm here, Iola."

Iola walked into the foyer and greeted Ashley. She grasped one of Ashley's hands and led her into the doll room, which seemed especially bright and full of life.

"I look forward to our visits so much, Ashley," Iola said. "I've never told these stories to anyone, and today I'm just about to burst!"

"I thought a lot about the little girl who gave the doll back, only to have it returned," Ashley said. "Yesterday I gave my cousin Lindsay one of my special doll dresses for no reason at all."

"That was a very nice thing to do, Ashley. Now let's see what Twadie has for us today." She picked up and handed Ashley a black doll with hair tied in several neat cornrows. Iola eagerly began her story:

About 70 years ago in Keystone, Oklahoma, a small farming town near the Arkansas River, a girl named Sheila lived with her parents and two younger brothers. Sheila was born blind, but that disability did not dim her inner spirit. She was renowned in Keystone for her bright personality, cheery disposition and infectious smile.

Sheila's loving parents and brothers did their best to make her life as happy as possible. Her father did seasonal work at a cotton gin and odd jobs at other times. The family lived simply, for money was always scarce.

Keystone was a typical small Southern town with a grocery and mercantile store, a bank, a blacksmith's shop and other businesses built around a tree-covered park in the town center. The churches near the center of town were heavily attended on Wednesday nights and Sunday mornings.

At this time in our nation's history, Keystone was segregated. White and black people went their separate ways. Only white people could drink from the water fountain in the town square. The white people lived on the high ground to the north of the square, and the black people lived in the swampy low lands near the river. The school for white children had a basketball court and indoor toilets. The black children went to a one-room school with no plumbing or electricity and an outdoor gymnasium. Most of the black people attended the one small church reserved for them. On the rare occasions when black people were invited into a white church, they sat in the rear balcony. Keystone was a quiet, safe town where people, traditionally separated by skin color, were civil to one another.

When the weather was nice, Sheila enjoyed sitting on a bench at the corner of the busiest intersection near the town square where she listened to the sounds of the people passing by. Over the years she learned to identify nearly everyone from the sound of their voices.

"Good morning, Mrs. Pierce." "Best of the day to you, Mr. Holdeman." She cheerfully greeted everyone walking past her.

And they returned her friendly salutations. Sheila was such a treasured fixture in the town square that many people, white and black, would go out of their way to exchange greetings with her.

Once a year all the residents of Keystone, black and white, gathered together in the town's largest church. On this occasion two magnificent porcelain dolls dressed in fancy clothes were given to the holders of winning raffle tickets. These unusually beautiful dolls, one white and the other black, could not be bought in stores, for they were handmade by a secret artist who donated them for this special event.

"That secret artist was me, Ashley," Iola said proudly, although Ashley had already guessed who made the dolls. Iola returned to her tale:

For 10 cents, a young girl could purchase a raffle ticket and place it in either of two large glass bowls. The winner of the white doll was drawn from one bowl, and the winner of the black doll was selected from the other. Each doll was placed in a white box tied with a bright ribbon.

Sheila had never had enough money to buy a raffle ticket until this year. She proudly paid the fee and received her ticket.

On the day of the raffle, always a Sunday after morning services, all the people of Keystone crowded into the large church to witness the drawing. Sheila and her family hurried to the church to find seats. Her ticket, number A047, was one of 200 in the bowl from which the white doll would be selected. Sheila and her family found seats near the back of the sanctuary. They were fortunate, for many people had to stand around the edges of the building and in the back hall.

The black people were crowded into the rear balcony overhead, and some had to stand outside and look in through the open windows. Finally the moment arrived, just in time to still the frantic squirming and hand wring-ing of several dozen little girls. The pastor stepped to the lectern and announced that he was ready to draw the winning number for the white doll. He reached into the bowl while looking upward and with a flourish pulled out the winning ticket. Without looking at the ticket, he motioned to a young boy sitting on the floor next to the lectern to come forward and read the winning number.

The lad studied the ticket carefully and then looked up at the pastor. His first words could not be heard.

"Speak up, son," urged the pastor.

The young man stretched to his full height, took a deep breath and shouted as loud as he could: "Number A-zero-four-seven. A-zero-four-seven."

There were murmurs in the room, and then Sheila cried out, "I have it! I have it! See, I have it!"

She stood, danced up and down and waved the ticket wildly in the air. Boisterous cheering and clapping in the lower and upper seats in the sanctuary and from out of doors filled the air when the audience realized that their beloved Sheila was the first winner. Sheila's mother gently led her daughter to the main aisle and to the front of the church where the pastor examined the ticket and verified that she had the winning number.

"I declare that Sheila is the winner of the white doll," he announced. "Please, bring the box to me."

An usher walked down the aisle with the large white box tied with an elegant ribbon and bow. He handed the box to Sheila, who was seated in a chair near the lectern. She was almost too excited to proceed. Her greatest wish had been answered. At last she would have a real doll.

She gently removed the ribbon and lifted the lid from the box. The doll was covered with delicate white tissue paper. Sheila lovingly slid her hands under the paper and began to examine her doll with sensitive fingers painting an image of her treasure behind eyes that could not see. She carefully explored the doll's arms and legs and dress, and then her face and hair, growing ever more excited as she bonded with her new friend.

I will name her Twadie, she thought, *after one of the nice ladies who speaks to me on the street corner.*

"Hold her up so that we can see her!" someone shouted.

Sheila reached into the box and grasped the doll, pulling it out of the box and to her chest in one easy motion.

There was a collective gasp from the audience and then stunned silence, as if all the people had suddenly been swept from the church with a giant broom.

After a few awkward moments someone spoke, "There's been a terrible mistake."

The people in the seats below and in the balcony above began to shift about uncomfortably and mumble excitedly to one another.

Then Sheila spoke out with tears streaming down her cheeks: "I want you all to meet my new best friend, Twadie. I love her so very much already. Thank you all for making this happen."

"You see, Ashley, Sheila had opened the box containing the black doll. How could she have known that her precious new friend was black? Someone had made a mistake. Or else the dolls had changed boxes, and who would believe that?" Iola said with a mischievous smile on her face. Then she resumed:

Without speaking, the pastor motioned for Sheila's parents to come to the front of the church. "This is a terrible mistake," he whispered. "Somehow the dolls got mixed up. I think we should exchange them now. Surely Sheila wants the white doll, doesn't she?"

"All we can do is ask her," Sheila's mother replied. "But I can see that Sheila has already bonded with this doll in her own special way. Although she cannot see the doll, she can picture her in her mind. If I know my daughter, she will probably not be satisfied with the other one."

"Well, let me try," the pastor responded. The audience was becoming restless.

The pastor approached Sheila and gently said, "Sheila, dear, we've had a bit of a mix up. You see, you were given the black doll by mistake, and we think that you might want to exchange her for the white one. Wouldn't you like to do that?"

Sheila sat quietly for a few moments, looking puzzled as she pondered the question. She pulled Twadie's face close to hers and gave her a long kiss on the cheek. Then she caressed her hair several times, smiling broadly as she spoke to the doll in inaudible words.

The pastor stood by helpless, unsure what to do next. Then Sheila turned and looked squarely in the direction of the pastor and asked in a voice loud enough for everyone inside and outside the church to hear, "Pastor, what is black?"

The perspiring pastor recoiled, placed one hand to his mouth and then spoke.

"Well, Sheila, you see—" He stopped abruptly and scolded himself, *You old fool, of course she can't see.*

After a moment of prayerful reflection that to some seemed an eternity, the pastor slowly stepped to the lectern and extended his upturned palms to the heavens. In a full and resonant voice, he said, "My brothers and sisters here below and in the balcony above, we have witnessed today the work of God Almighty spoken in the voice and lived in the spirit of this beautiful child. Though young Sheila cannot see as you and I do, she has a truer vision of our soul's inner spirit than any of us with two good eyes. For the love of God is blind to the color of our skin, a difference between us that too often leads to hatred and bitterness in a world that would be better served by acceptance. Oh, that we should all be as gifted as our beloved Sheila!"

Looking up at the people in the balcony, the pastor then asked, "Shall we proceed with the next drawing?"

There was the sound of hushed conversations as heads turned from side to side. Then the people in the balcony nodded and a few said, "Yes, YES," as a new spirit of expectation began to rise.

The white doll was won by a dark-skinned girl named Addie, who at that moment took her turn to be the happiest little girl on earth. And in the days that followed, all of the people of Keystone walked on both sides of the street together, shared the drinking fountain in the park and sat together in the churches as though that was the way it had been for all time.

And Sheila grew to be a fine woman who faithfully sat at her corner in the center of town with Twadie one day each week to greet the people of Keystone.

"Iola, how did the dolls get mixed up on that special day?" Ashley asked.

"Well, Ashley, that mystery still puzzles the citizens of Keystone and the communities nearby. Only Twadie knows for sure."

"Will Twadie tell you, Iola?" Ashley asked.

"She is a terrible tease, Ashley. Perhaps one day."

As the enchantment of Iola's story began to lift, Ashley realized that she had stayed later than usual.

"Oh my! I've got to go home. I'll see you tomorrow," she said as she raced toward the front door.

"Until tomorrow," Iola replied, waving slowly as her young friend ran down the path to Windsor Drive.

CHAPTER THIRTEEN

Mediocre Man

$\mathcal{A}$SHLEY WAS RUNNING OUT of excuses to tell her friends, so on this day she walked with them all the way home and then turned around and ran as fast as she could back to Iola's house. Iola was waiting as usual, the front door ajar. These visits had become so routine that Ashley let herself in, announcing her arrival from the foyer. Iola was seated in the magical room with two dolls on her lap, a brother and sister duo known to professional dollmakers today as Peaches and Patches.

"Welcome, Ashley," Iola greeted. "I want you to meet Connor and Emily. They are brother and sister. I made them about 30 years ago, and they have just returned home. Since they are brother and sister dolls, I arranged for them to always be together."

"They are so cute! Where have they been?" Ashley asked as she cradled the dolls in her arms and settled on the floor for Iola's story.

Connor and Emily spent all of their time in Pratt, a small town in the south central part of Kansas. I gave them to a little girl in Prairie Village named Janeane, who moved a short time later to Pratt. Janeane had three younger brothers,

Taylor, Aaron and Joel. Janeane was nine years old, as I recall, and her brothers were about eight, seven and six. They lived in a small house on the west side of Pratt. Their father was a milkman who never met a stranger. Their mother kept the home, raised chickens and always planted a large garden. Janeane, being the oldest child in the family, was expected to keep her brothers in line, which turned out to be an impossible task.

The boys were very adventuresome. Taylor had established a club called the Mediocre Man Club. He was The Man, which was the highest ranking in the club. Conveniently, he was the only one who could ever hold that elite title. The younger brothers were eligible to be in the club but at a lower rank. If they passed certain initiation rites set up by Taylor, they could become a Piglet, the first level of membership, and then a Mediocre Man, the second level.

Piglet initiation rites included picking up Taylor's clothes and hanging them in the closet, giving him their desserts, especially when they had strawberry shortcake or ice cream and cake, and carrying his books to school.

They also were called on to torment their older sister. She found them non-cooperative when she handed out instructions from their parents. Her hairbrush and curlers would mysteriously disappear, and secret notes from her school friends would appear taped to the refrigerator door. The younger brothers met these tests in a couple of months and advanced to the rank of Piglet.

The tests to become a Mediocre Man were more severe. To begin with, they had to swim naked in an icy stream in the middle of winter. The nearest stream was about two miles from their house. To get there, the brothers had to walk along the railroad tracks to a bridge that crossed the stream as it meandered through a wooded ravine. The stream had cut a deep gorge, leaving large boulders exposed along either side. The rocks were partially obscured by large cottonwood trees that had been growing there for more than 100 years.

Taylor had discovered this place the summer before with some neighbor friends. They had found a swimming hole that had been hollowed out beneath the railroad trestle, and they named the hole the Black Pool. No one else—least of all their parents—knew of this mysterious rocky place hidden among the overhanging trees.

Aaron and Joel sneaked out of the house early one freezing winter morning under Taylor's leadership and headed for the Black Pool and their first major test toward becoming a Mediocre Man. Their feet crunched on the frosty gravel along the tracks until they arrived at the railroad bridge and carefully descended along a narrow trail into the gorge. They could see downstream for about a hundred yards as the water wound its way beyond the Black Pool.

"Okay, Aaron, you're the oldest, so you go first," Taylor instructed from the water's edge.

"How long do I have to stay in?" Aaron asked.

"Until The Man says you can get out!" Taylor replied with high authority.

Aaron hesitated at first and then slowly removed all his clothes. Standing there naked he began to shiver, as the sun, just peaking over the rim of the gorge, gave no relief from the morning chill. Aaron stuck one great toe in the frigid waters and then yanked it out. He looked at his older brother, who stared back intently while shaking his head in disapproval. On the second attempt, Aaron got his right foot in the water and then his whole leg. Suddenly his left foot slipped on the slick embankment, and he fell into the water with a mighty splash. The water only came to his chest but he thrashed around, doing his best to spray his brothers with the frigid, murky water.

"Come on in, Joel! The water's fine," Aaron yelled to his younger brother. Then addressing Taylor, he asked, "This enough?"

Taylor stroked his chin for several moments and then replied, "Head under water for 10 counts."

Aaron complied and then asked permission to get out.

"Two more times will do," Taylor instructed.

After meeting that test, Aaron got out of the water and quickly stripped as much of the water off as he could and put on his clothes and coat, shivering so hard he could not speak.

"Okay, Joel, your turn," Taylor ordered.

Joel looked at his miserable brother and then at the murky waters of the Black Pool and said meekly, "I think I'll pass this time."

"You know what this means, Piglet!" Taylor scorned. "You're not going to be a Mediocre Man very soon."

Joel dropped his head and uttered a faint, "Yes, I know."

The boys climbed back up to the railroad tracks and began walking at a brisk pace. Aaron's teeth chattered all the way home in rhythm with their steps.

Their mother, who had awakened early on this weekend morning had not missed the boys, assuming they were sleeping in. Seeing them traipse into the house, she became alarmed at the sight of the blue, shivering Aaron.

"Where in the world have you boys been? Good grief, Aaron, how did you get so wet?" she asked, her arms akimbo and a scowl on her face. With three active sons, she was accustomed to surprises when one of their frequent adventures backfired. But this looked more serious.

Taylor spoke up before Aaron could utter a sound through his chattering teeth. "We just went for a walk down the street. Aaron was goofing around and fell into Mr. Olsen's horse watering trough in the pasture."

Joel struggled to keep a straight face as Taylor spun his tale.

"Well, it's freezing outside today. Let's get you into a hot bath right away. After you're warm and dry, you three can help your sister with the chores today. I have given her a list that she will share with you when she gets up."

The chilling experience in the Black Pool dampened Joel's interest in becoming a Mediocre Man. Being a Piglet forever was okay with him. He would be satisfied to amuse himself by watching his determined brother try to achieve his impossible goal.

In the spring, when the leaves had popped out and the days were warming up, Aaron asked Taylor what he would have to do next to become a Mediocre Man. Taylor was ready for him.

"What does Janeane treasure more than anything in the world?" Taylor asked.

"Her dolls, Connor and Emily," Aaron immediately replied.

"Then you've got to steal 'em and hide 'em in the Wind Cave near the Black Pool," Taylor demanded.

The Wind Cave was about 200 yards downstream

from the Black Pool. The boys had discovered the cave entrance the preceding summer. It had a rounded entrance, about three feet across, that was framed by several large boulders. Some, just a few feet above the opening, looked wobbly. The entrance expanded into a small room just tall enough at the center for Taylor to stand up. The boys had fashioned a drape over the inside of the entrance, making the cave completely dark. They kept candles and some matches hidden in the cave to illuminate their special meetings of the Mediocre Man Club.

"Gosh, Taylor. This is pretty serious stuff," Aaron said. "Isn't there something else I could do?"

"The Man has spoken, Piglet! Do you wish to be a Piglet forever?" Taylor asked pompously as Joel hid a gigantic smile with his hands and started coughing to disguise his laughter.

On Saturday morning before the sun had risen, Aaron sneaked into Janeane's room and took Connor and Emily from their makeshift crib. He tiptoed out of the room and through the kitchen to the back yard where Taylor and Joel met him. The three brothers walked quietly to the railroad track and then skipped along the timbers, amusing themselves with several versions of how they imagined their bossy sister would react to the disappearance of her precious dolls. When they arrived at the Black Pool, Aaron tossed the dolls under some bushes and walked to the water's edge.

Recalling his freezing initiation during the winter, he turned to Joel and asked pointedly, "Okay, Piglet—Weenie—are you ever going to take the next step to become a Mediocre Man?"

"I'm thinking about it," Joel replied, afraid that a grin would appear on his face and give away his scheme. "Next winter for sure, Aaron."

"Let's go look at the cave first and find a good place to put the dolls," Taylor called as he raced downstream.

The boys ran to the cave entrance and looked in. All was clear. Taylor entered first, followed by Aaron and Joel. They found the candles and lit one. Taylor draped the cave entrance, and they all sat down on the sandy floor around the candle to decide where they would put the dolls. As they sat quietly for a few moments, the dim light from the flickering candle cast their ghostly shadows on the rocky walls behind them. The eerie silence was broken by the high-pitched wail of a whistle as a locomotive approached the trestle spanning the Black Pool.

Suddenly, the ground beneath them and the rock walls on either side of the cave began to shake as a mighty freight train rumbled over the bridge. One of the boulders perched above the cave's entrance shook loose after having been teased by passing trains for many years. The giant rock smashed to the ground, scoring a bull's-eye on the opening to the cave. One of the boys lurched forward, knocking the candle over and putting it out. The boys immediately found themselves enveloped in the blackest dark they'd ever seen.

"What was that?" Joel asked.

"Something fell outside," Taylor replied.

Simultaneously, the boys crawled toward the cave entrance and in a tangle of arms and legs, they yanked the drape off. But the blackest dark remained.

"Something is blocking the entrance!" Taylor shouted. "Feels like one of those big boulders."

Calmly, Taylor crawled back to the center of the cave

and found the candle and the matches. With a shaky hand, he struck a match. But the shaft broke in two, and the match did not ignite. He found another match, which this time burst into flame as he struck it. He lit the candle, revealing his trembling brothers with their arms around each other.

"Here. You hold the light, Aaron. I'll push the rock away," Taylor instructed calmly.

Taylor knelt down and placed both hands on the rock and pushed with all his might. The stone didn't budge. He tried again and again, grunting and straining each time. Taylor was large for his age, and when his brothers saw that he could not budge the stone, they realized that they were in big trouble.

"Guess you guys are going to have to help," Taylor yelled out to his fellow club members.

Together they dug their feet into the sandy cave floor and pushed on the boulder, straining and grunting. But the stone would not move. They tried sitting with their backs to the stone and pushing with their legs until their feet burrowed deeply into the sand. Still the stone didn't move. They were trapped, a long way from home, and no one knew where they were.

"Wha–whadwe d–do now?" Joel asked, his voice giving away the fear he felt rising with the lump in his throat.

"Try to stay calm. We can figure this out," Taylor replied.

"I'm getting scared too," Aaron interjected. "I guess we're getting what we deserve. Oh shoot! I left the dolls out there. Dang, they'll get dirty!"

Taylor didn't respond, as fear had begun to grip him too. Only a few of their neighborhood friends knew about the cave. They could be stuck for a long time without food and water. Eventually the candles would run out, and they would be trapped in the dark.

"We've got to have a plan," Taylor finally said as calmly as he could. "Surely someone will come to the Black Pool today. We should yell as loud as we can every so often so they can hear us."

So they yelled, whooped and hollered as loudly as they could every 10 or 15 minutes for several hours. Although no one came, the physical exertion of yelling relieved some of the tension and fear.

Taylor counted the matches and the candles. He figured that they had three or four hours of light left and that by rationing the candles and matches, they would be able to see one another and the interior of the cave for several days, if necessary.

Janeane awoke and sat up in bed, rubbing the sleep out of her eyes. As part of her daily ritual, she turned to say good morning to Connor and Emily. They were gone.

Mother must have taken them, she thought.

She rushed into the kitchen and said, "Mom, do you have Connor and Emily?"

"Why, no. Are they missing from your room?"

"They're gone! They were there when I went to bed last night."

"Well, look around. I'm sure you'll find them somewhere."

Janeane looked in every room and every closet. She did not find her dolls. "Mom, where are my brothers?" she asked, tightly clamping her jaws together.

"Aren't they in their room?"

"No. They are not anywhere, and I'll bet they know where my dolls are. Those skunks are up to something."

"I'll get your father, and we'll see where the boys are. Get dressed, and we'll figure this all out," Mother instructed calmly.

Janeane and her parents looked everywhere in the house and yard for the boys. They yelled out their names but got no response. Her father visited neighbors where the boys played and asked if anyone knew where they were. No one did, but Joel's close friend John volunteered that they might be at the Black Pool. He knew that they liked to go there, and he agreed to show them the way.

"My throat's getting sore from yelling," Aaron said huskily. "Can't you think of anything else, The Man?"

"I'm sorry for getting you guys into this. The whole idea was pretty dumb," Taylor replied.

"We went along with it. We didn't have to," Joel said. "I've been thinking a lot about Neanie. What has she done to deserve all the things we've done to her?"

"She's a little prissy and bossy, but I guess that's not a crime. I'd sure like to see her now, and Mom and Dad," Aaron said, a lump creeping into his throat.

"Hang on, guys. We'll get out of this. Just keep thinking— and yelling. Come on now—together—Whaaaaaa Yahooooo Whaaaaaaaa!"

Janeane, her parents and John reached the railroad tracks and started toward the bridge. Janeane spotted a small white object between two of the timbers the steel rails were fastened to. She bent down and picked it up.

"Mom! Dad! It's Connor's shoe. We're on the right track."

"Indeed, Janeane, we *are* on the right tracks," her father replied with a chuckle.

They found another shoe about a mile away from the first. The shoes evidently had fallen off Connor as the boys skipped along the timbers. Janeane and the others reached the bridge and walked down the path to the Black Pool, where they found Connor and Emily on the bank near the water, lying face up, each with their right arms extended in the same direction, downstream. Janeane raced to pick them up, but her father stopped her.

"They seem to be pointing in that direction, Janeane. Do you think that could mean anything?" her father asked.

"I don't know. John, what do you know about this place? Is there another hideout or something else downstream?"

John shrugged his shoulders, since he did not know about the Wind Cave.

"Janeane, you pick up the dolls, and let's all walk slowly downstream. I'll call out to the boys as we go along."

"Taylor! Aaron! Joel!" Father yelled as he walked beside the stream.

They had walked about 50 paces when Father stopped abruptly and put his finger to his lips to quiet the others. "I thought I heard a yell," he said softly. They all strained to hear something. "There, I heard it again, just a bit ahead of us." Father started running along the stream yelling at the top of his lungs. The other yelling became stronger, and he localized it to the stone blocking the cave's entrance.

"Are you guys in there?" he called from beside the boulder.

"Yes! Yes! Yippee! HOOOOrah!" he heard coming from the other side of the boulder.

"It's Mom, Dad, Janeane and John out here," he called to his sons. "Stay calm. We're going to get you out."

Their father strained to move the boulder, but it was stuck tight and wouldn't budge.

"Watch out!" their mother screamed as another loose boulder began to fall. Their father jumped aside just as the

87

rock crashed to the ground inches away from his foot. He looked briefly at the fallen rock next to his foot and then to the steep ledge above to see if any more greeters might drop in on him.

"Close call!" he yelled. "I'll need a pole to wedge this thing out."

Their father disappeared for a few minutes, and in his absence Janeane and her mother spoke loudly at either edge of the huge boulder to reassure the trapped boys. Their father returned shortly with a stout fence post, one end of which he wedged between the boulder and the cave entrance. Using the post as a lever, he pushed on the end with all his power. The boulder budged half an inch. He pushed again, and then again. Each time the boulder moved a bit more.

Finally, a boy's hand reached out of the narrow opening and gave a thumb's-up sign. A few more grunts, and the opening was wide enough for the boys to squeeze out of the cave and into the eager arms of their parents and sister. With the sudden relief that freedom brings, the boys of the Mediocre Man Club began to wail at the top of their lungs.

In a few minutes, the tears slowed enough for Taylor to ask, "How did you ever find us?"

"The dolls led us to you, with a little help from John," Janeane replied. "Connor lost both of his shoes along the railroad tracks, and that proved you had a) stolen my dolls and b) come this way," she said with mock scorn.

"We're sorry Neanie, really sorry," the boys said in unison.

"I accept your apology, pests," she answered, and she hugged them again. "By the way, you sure were smart to leave the dolls out in the open pointing toward the cave."

The boys looked in disbelief at one another before Aaron replied, "Neanie, that's not where I left them. I dropped them on the side of the path, under a bush."

Ashley was exhausted after hearing the saga of Connor and Emily. "Those boys were in great danger, weren't they?" she asked Iola.

"Indeed they were," Iola answered. "But I bet they treated their sister with a little more respect after that."

"How did the dolls manage to give the signal to Janeane and her parents?"

"Another secret, Ashley, another secret. You know, I feel very tired today. I'm afraid I'm not going to have enough time to tell you about all of my friends and their travels," Iola said as she looked about the room wistfully. "So much has happened. We should hear from Addison, Allissa and Dillon. They've brought so much happiness to so many. But I'm very tired, my dear, very tired. Now go along, and do come back tomorrow."

Ashley kissed Iola's forehead, gave her a gentle hug and walked slowly to the door, very confused—and a bit concerned—about Iola's parting words.

CHAPTER FOURTEEN
Disappearing act

SATURDAY MORNING, 6 a.m., and everyone in the house was asleep but Ashley. Her last meeting with Iola had disturbed her. Why didn't Iola have time for all the stories? Was she planning to go away?

Ashley got dressed, gulped down a glass of apple juice and bounded out of the house toward Iola's place. The sun was peeking over the trees on the east side of Windsor Drive, illuminating a crystalline, dew-kissed morning meant for magic.

She ran through the open iron gate to Iola's house and onto the porch. She let herself into the front door and called for her friend.

There was no answer. She called louder, but there still was no answer.

Iola told me she's always awake early, Ashley thought, her concern growing.

She walked to the doll room where she and Iola had met so many times before.

"Oh my!" she blurted out. "The dolls are gone! Iola! Iola!"

The room was completely empty. There was no sign of a doll anywhere.

Maybe she was robbed–a prowler, she thought as she anxiously circled the room.

Ashley ran to the bedroom, but Iola's bed was empty and neatly made. She ran to the back door, which was ajar, and looked into the yard that was still darkened by the canopy of large trees.

She saw a narrow pathway leading deeper into this little forest on Windsor Drive, the only place in the city where dozens of 100-year-old trees stretched to the heavens to create a sanctuary below.

Ashley followed the path into the forest, where she was greeted by the delicious fragrance of incense. A few feet farther and the path entered a cathedral-like opening. In the center of this forest-shrouded room lay Iola on a bed of clean golden straw, adorned with fresh-cut flowers and surrounded by all of her dolls.

"Iola, what are you doing here?" Ashley asked timidly as she stepped toward the motionless old lady.

Iola's eyes were closed. She lay perfectly still on the straw, her dolls in silent vigil around her.

"Iola, please don't play tricks on me! Please don't!" Ashley pleaded.

Iola did not move.

Iola's hands were folded across her chest. In her right hand was an envelope with the inscription "To Ashley" written on it. Ashley cautiously approached Iola and gently pulled the envelope from her hand. She sat beside her beloved Iola, opened the letter and read aloud:

Dear Ashley,
    Please do not be afraid or concerned. I am enjoy-

92

*ing a much-needed rest here in this beautiful place.
I think my time will come fairly soon, and I'm ready
to let go. Take the ring from my finger, and place it
on one of the fingers of your right hand. Place this
hand on top of mine, close your eyes and think of
the most special thought you can imagine. You will
feel the power of the ring flow from me to you. You
will soon discover that you possess the powers that I
have told you about during our visits. I know that
you will always respect the power of this ring.*

Ashley couldn't believe that Iola was giving her the
magical ring. But neither could she refuse Iola's request.
She carefully removed from Iola's finger the golden ring
with the large opal and put it on the first finger of her
right hand. Then she placed her hand over Iola's as she
had been instructed. Ashley closed her eyes and thought
of the times that she and Iola had met to recount the
dolls' stories.

She soon felt the ring warm her finger. Then her
entire right hand became so hot that she had to lift it
away from Iola. Through her closed eyelids, she could
see an intense blue-white light illuminating the cathedral
beneath the trees. Then she heard the sweet harmonies
of a children's choir singing a joyous song of praise that
echoed through this beautiful, mysterious place in the
heart of the small forest. The singing seemed to come
from around where Iola lay, but the dolls were motionless.

As Ashley opened her eyes, she saw the opal ring
blazing intensely. Bright sunlight, streaming through
small portholes in the umbrella of tree branches over-

head, fell as beacons on Iola, the dolls and Ashley. This was a magical moment, indeed.

With tears in her eyes, Ashley read on:

Now you must leave me. There is a box near my feet. It contains a deed to this property, which I now give to you. This, dearest Ashley, is my gift in return for your precious company and kindness to me. But I do ask one favor. Please leave me alone here with my friends. All will be well. As you leave, be sure to close the iron gate and latch it securely. Please don't come back here for at least one day.

I trust you to do just as I say. You are now free to tell your parents about the ring and your magic powers. Come back in a day with your father and mother and tell them exactly what you found and what you did. This letter will be your proof.

And so goodbye, sweet Ashley.

Yours forever,

Iola

Ashley folded the letter and put it in a pocket of her dress. She found the box at Iola's feet, opened it and found the deed just as Iola had said she would. She looked again at Iola lying there. She was in a deep, happy sleep.

How did she arrange all of this last night? Ashley wondered. *She must have had some help, but who?*

The music seemed louder as Ashley walked out of the clearing and onto the cloistered path that led back to Iola's house. She passed through the house, taking care to close the doors behind her. At the front gate, she grabbed the iron door firmly and shut and latched it in one sharp CLANG! It was as though this sound was the signal for the singers to raise their voices in a furious crescendo, which then slowly died away to a faint unison chorus of Iola's theme song: "Who's afraid of the wicked witch, the wicked witch of Windsor?"

In the silence of the morning, Ashley walked home with the box Iola had given her and, for the rest of the day, sat on the porch swing speaking to no one.

CHAPTER FIFTEEN

Talking dolls?

MORNING LIGHT streamed into Ashley's room with unusual brightness. On this day she could finally tell her parents about Iola's wonderful stories and about the Mooncorn People. Ashley ran to her parent's room and jumped into their bed, awakening them with a start.

"What on earth is going on, Ashley?" her mother asked sleepily.

Her father pulled a pillow over his head and rolled to the edge of the bed.

"You can't escape me, Daddy. I've got wonderful news! Wake up!" she shouted as she shook him with all of her strength.

"Okay, Okay," he replied gruffly. "But go plug in the coffee pot."

Ashley ran to the kitchen to get the coffee started and to put bread in the toaster. A few moments later Ashley and her parents were seated at the breakfast table, and she began her long and animated tale of her adventures on Windsor Drive.

She started with the Mooncorn People. How Willa Hauptman had buried them in the Mason jar her dad found under the tree stump in their back yard and that the cryptic note had referred to two tiny people who had escaped from the jar when it was broken.

"Ashley," her mother interrupted, "we have known for some time that you have a rich imagination, but it's awfully early in the morning for your dad and me to be listening to your fairy tales."

"Mom, it's true. It's true. It's all true!" Ashley insisted, her voice growing louder with each declaration. "Please just sit here and let me tell you the rest. I promise I'm not making any of this up."

Her parents stole bewildered glances at one another. Shaking his head slowly, her father said, "Okay, Ashley, go on. You can tell us your story, but you must understand that your mom and I find this more than a little hard to believe."

"There's a lot more, and I have some things to show you." Ashley began. She told them about the magic mooncorn seeds and the problems she had growing them. How she gave the ears of corn to Tork and Marie, who then regained their normal size. How she figured out that Elie and Nicole were buried under Louie's oak tree and how she freed them, found their parents and sent them on their way back to Belgium.

"Ashley, I've just about had enough of this," her mother said impatiently. "I've got a mountain of work to do today, and your dad needs to mow the grass. Can't this wait until another time?"

Tears began to well up in Ashley's eyes as she realized that neither of her parents believed a word of her story.

"Oh Mommy, Daddy, please believe me," she pleaded. "I've just got to tell you about Iola and the gifts she gave me yesterday. Oh, please listen some more."

Seeing their daughter so upset about their disbelief, they nodded to each other, a signal that they should let their daughter have some more time to tell this story that meant so much to her.

"Okay, Ashley," her mother said as she poured more coffee and settled again in her chair. "We will listen to the rest."

Beginning anew, Ashley told of her frequent meetings with Iola, of Iola and Willa's friendship and, very briefly, the stories of each doll's adventure. Then she carefully explained the events of the day before, her last visit with Iola, and showed them the box containing the deed.

Her father examined the deed for several minutes. "I find it hard to believe, Ashley, but this is a wonderful gift from your friend. And it looks perfectly legal to me."

"That's not all. She gave me this special ring, the one she got from Willa Hauptman, the good gypsy I told you about." She held out her hand so that her parents could inspect the ring.

"It's lovely, Ashley," her mother said as she studied the ring. "And does it have magical powers?"

"Iola said it would. I felt a strangely warm tingle in my arm when I first put it on, and then, when I put my hand on top of hers, I felt a stronger heat. I also saw a gorgeous glow in the forest that lasted for several minutes. The note in the box says that I am to bring you both to her house today. See. Read it for yourselves." She thrust Iola's hand-written note in front of her parents. "I think we should go back to Iola's house right now to see if she is still there in the forest. I'm very concerned about her. I hope she's all right."

They woke up Josh, and he staggered along after them as they hurried down Windsor Drive to Iola's house. Nothing appeared to have changed in front of the house. Ashley led them to the front door, opened it and called for Iola. No one answered. Ashley entered as she had done the day before, and her parents and Josh followed. There was still no answer to her call for Iola. Ashley went to the back door, opened it and led her parents along the narrow path to the opening in the forest. She had no idea what she would encounter but, knowing Iola, she anticipated some kind of a surprise. In the center of the opening, where Iola had lain surrounded by her dolls, sat one lonely doll–Julie, the first doll Iola had made. Ashley ran to her and clutched her to her chest. After a vigorous hug, she held the doll at arm's length.

"Oh, Julie!" Ashley exclaimed. "Everyone else is gone without a trace. What has happened, Julie? Where's Iola?"

She sat Julie on the ground and joined her parents to look about the clearing for clues to the disappearance of Ashley's friend and the other dolls. Josh stood motionless, staring intently at Julie, a bewildered look on his sleepy face. Ashley's father turned to her and said, "I can't find any evidence of foul play here, Ashley. I think your friend Iola was very organized and had planned everything well ahead. She must have arranged for someone to come here and take her and the dolls away."

Ashley wasn't sure her father's explanation accounted for everything, but there was nothing else she could do. Ashley picked Julie up, and together they all walked back through the house and to the front gate where this great adventure had begun.

"Mom, would you and Daddy take Josh and go on ahead? I want to say goodbye once more," Ashley said with sadness in her voice.

"Sure, Ashley. Take as much time as you need."

Ashley walked slowly back into the house and stood for several minutes in the empty doll room, echoes of Iola's stories rattling around in her head. Then she left through the front door, closing it behind her. In the front yard she found one of the sticks that she and her friends used to drag along the fence on their way to and from school. She walked to the far end of the block and, with Julie draped over her left shoulder, she skipped up Windsor Drive as the stick struck the iron bars to the beat of "Who's afraid of the wicked witch, the wicked witch of Windsor?"

When she reached the end of the fence, she placed the stick behind the iron bars, turned toward Iola's house and sighed, "It's been so wonderful. I'll miss you all so much, so very much."

As tears flooded her cheeks, she heard a small voice whisper in her left ear, "Ashley, I have so much to tell you."

CHAPTER SIXTEEN

What's Julie up to?

ASHLEY STOPPED WALKING and held Julie directly in front of her.

"Julie, did you just talk to me? Tell me I have magic powers."

Julie was silent, the faint smile on her porcelain lips unchanged.

"Come on, Julie. I know you're a tease. Did you say something to me, like, 'Ashley I have so much to tell you?'"

Julie remained silent, smiling.

When she reached her yard, she found Joshua, now wide awake, riding his scooter up and down the driveway to the garage.

"Who gave ya the doll, Ash?"

"A lady gave it to me."

"She looks breakable. Is she a breakable doll?"

"Yes, she is, and you'd better keep your toy-breaker hands off of her."

"Geeze, Ash. I get blamed for everything around here. I even got blamed for the mud you dragged in the house from that stupid corn garden."

"Just take it easy, Buster," Ashley said in mock anger

as she bent down to kiss the forehead of her younger brother.

Ashley went into the kitchen where her parents were in conversation over coffee.

"Well, I see you made it back all right with Julie. You must be feeling a little blue, right Ashley?" her mother inquired as she gave her daughter a hug.

"Ash, what in the world are we going to do with that big old house Mrs. Taylor gave you?" her father asked.

Ashley shrugged her shoulders as she looked down at Julie cradled in her arms.

"Oh well, we'll not worry about it just now. Something will pop up," her father said.

"You know, I just can't imagine what happened to all of Iola's dolls, and to Iola," Ashley said. "I told you that she had magic powers and that she could talk to those dolls. Every one of them had been given to a little girl, and when the girl was finished with them they found their way back to Iola and they told her every-thing they had seen and heard. Iola had dozens and dozens of dolls and as many stories. She only got to tell me three of them before she disappeared. But she left Julie, her first doll, and she knows all of the stories. Now I have to persuade her to tell them to me."

Ashley's parents stared across the breakfast table at one another, speechless. "I think we may have a prob-lem in the making," her mother whispered to her hus-band.

"Ashley, what makes you think that Iola could talk to the dolls?" her mother asked calmly.

"Well, she told me she did, and Iola wouldn't lie.

You just wait and see."

"You know, Ashley, almost every little girl has talked to her dolls, but they don't expect them to talk back. Have you ever heard them speak to you?" her mother asked.

"I think so, but I'm not sure."

"Look, why don't you just keep this talking doll business our little secret for awhile. I wouldn't talk to anyone about it, or it might break the spell," her mother said, not realizing that this advice to protect her daughter from ridicule was just what Ashley needed in order to keep her powers.

"Ashley, your doll experience is such a neat story," her father added.

"It did happen, Mom, Dad. Look, Iola gave me this magic ring that gives me the power to talk to dolls."

Her parents looked briefly at the ring but did not think for a moment that it had magic powers.

"If you say this all happened, then in your heart it did. You've had a very exciting week, Ashley, and I think you should put Julie in your room for awhile and find some of your old friends to play with."

I'm not getting anywhere with my parents, Ashley thought, *so I'd better lay low for awhile.*

She took Julie to her room and placed her at the head of her bed, leaning her against the wall. Ashley stood at the side of the bed for several minutes looking intently at Julie's smiling face.

"I think you're playing one of your tricks on me, Miss Julie. I've just got that feeling."

CHAPTER SEVENTEEN

Magic meets reality

WEEKS PASSED, and the sumptuous colors of fall began to fade as leaves floated to the ground in increasing numbers. Julie did not speak, and Ashley tried every conceivable trick to get the doll to open up. Dances in the back yard late at night. Parades through Iola's house. Runs through Iola's back yard. Threats, sweet talk, tears, screaming.

Nothing worked.

Frustration grew and grew because Ashley wanted so desperately to know what had happened to Iola and her dolls. *They couldn't just vanish into thin air. Making dolls talk was one thing, but making everyone disappear without a trace was too much to accept,* she thought.

Julie's refusal to speak to her caused Ashley to back away from trying to convince her parents that she had been given magic powers or that the story she had told them was in fact true. Mr. and Mrs. Houchin were relieved that this "talking doll and tiny people" phase of Ashley's life had finally passed.

Ashley began to wonder if Iola had played a big trick on her, as her mother had once intimated. After all, Ashley had never heard the dolls speak. All she had to go on was Iola's stories and those few words she thought Julie might have whispered into her ear. Was that just the wind? And the magic ring? Maybe it had a secret battery inside that made it glow and heat up that day in the forest behind Iola's house. Yes, maybe this was just a sweet old lady who knew Willa Hauptman and made up this talking doll thing.

Yet the Dubois family was for real, as was their mooncorn magic. Ashley resolved to be patient with Julie. She probably had a plan up her sleeve.

Late one cold December Saturday afternoon Ashley entered her room to find *The Johnson County Squire* newspaper folded neatly on her bed. She unfolded it and read the front page banner headline:

Country Court celebrates 106th birthday of oldest resident

Ashley stared at the picture below the headline. There she was as clear as life—Iola Taylor! She read the picture caption to be certain: "Iola Taylor, a lifelong resident of Johnson County, will celebrate her 106th birthday on January 3."

Ashley grabbed the paper and ran into the kitchen.

"Mom, did you put this paper on my bed?"

"No."

"Did Dad?"

"I wouldn't think so. He's been at work all day."

"How about Josh? Has he been in my room lately?"

"He's innocent. He's been at a friend's house all day."

"Look, Mom. It's Iola. Iola! She's living in Country Court, whatever that is."

Her mother took the paper from Ashley and looked intently at the picture.

"Isn't that wonderful, Ashley? You've found her. I think the Country Court is a retirement home quite a ways south of here. I wonder why she didn't tell you she was moving there?" her mother asked.

"That lady is certainly full of surprises," Ashley said joyously. Then her mood quieted and her face saddened. "I wonder if she'll let me see her. Will you take me there today, Mom? Please. Please!"

"Kind of late for an unscheduled visit, Ash."

"Oh, please, Mom. I miss her so much," she pleaded as she walked slowly around her mother with hands poised as in prayer.

Her mother's face smiled in surrender. "Ash, I've been around you enough to know that you will never give up on this. Let me brush my hair and put on a dress. You should straighten yourself up as well."

Ashley bounced into her room and started to change her clothes. As she was pulling off her T-shirt, she heard a girl's laughter coming from the head of the bed.

"Tee, hee, hee!"

Ashley jerked the shirt over her head and whirled to see who was laughing. All she saw was Julie with that everlasting smile on her face.

"So you're behind this! Someday will I ever get even with you!" Ashley said as she regained confidence in her promised magic powers. "Julie, I'm going to see Iola, and I shouldn't take you with me, just for spite. But I can't do that. It wouldn't be fair to Iola."

She flung Julie over her shoulder and headed

toward the kitchen.

"Don't be so sore with me, Ashley. You'll see that everything is going to work out just fine," Julie whispered into her ear.

A smile grew huge across Ashley's face.

The trip to Country Court seemed to take forever. The winter sun was setting behind some high clouds in the southwest, and slivers of reddish gold light gave the heavens a luminescent radiance. Ashley and her mom parked the car and walked through the main entrance on the north end of the building. The entry foyer opened to a long, dimly lit hallway where, on either side, Ashley saw long rows of benches and chairs with people sitting on them. Silver-haired, elderly women and a few men all interrupted their conversations to look at the unexpected guests walking by.

The diffused light of the evening sunset, entering through large glass windows at the south end of the hallway, illuminated the people of Country Court in a mystic glow, reminding Ashley of that charmed moment when she entered Iola's parlor for the first time to find herself surrounded by lifelike porcelain dolls. Only this time the dolls were alive and had begun to move and whisper to one another as the curiosity of visitors broke up the tedium of their day.

At the reception area, Ashley's mother spoke to the attendant. "I'm Mrs. Houchin, and this is my daughter, Ashley. We've come to see Mrs. Iola Taylor, a friend of Ashley's."

"Yes," replied the attendant, "Mrs. Taylor is expecting you."

"Expecting us? How could that be?" Ashley's mother asked.

Ashley tugged on her mother's sleeve and shook her head, hoping to keep her from talking so much.

"All I know is that her caregiver notified the desk today that Ashley Houchin would be here to see her and that she was very welcome," the receptionist said.

Ashley motioned for her mother to lean down so she could whisper into her ear.

"Mom, this is kind of complicated. But I promise, I'll tell you all about it as soon as I can."

Just then Ashley heard another "Tee, hee, hee" coming from Julie.

"Okay, Ash," her mother replied. "But ya know, I'm supposed to be the adult here, you amazing child."

The attendant led Ashley and her mother to a room in the assisted living section of Country Court. She paused outside Iola's room and said, "I suppose that you know that she will not be able to see you. She has completely lost her eyesight. I wouldn't stay too long. She tires easily."

Ashley tapped on the door three times.

From behind the door she heard Iola's weak voice say, "Come in, Ashley."

Another "Tee, hee, hee" came from Julie.

Ashley, her mother and Julie entered the dimly lit room to find Iola sitting up in bed looking in their direction. She held out both of her arms, motioning Ashley to come to her.

Ashley ran several steps, then paused and walked slowly, taking care to embrace Iola warmly without hurting her.

"Oh, Ashley, my dear sweet Ashley. How I've missed you. And Julie, I heard that naughty giggle of yours."

Ashley's mother turned and looked curiously at Julie.

"I've missed you too, Iola, more than I could ever tell you," Ashley said.

Ashley's mother moved closer to the bed.

"Iola, my mother is with me. I think you know her."

"Indeed I do. Hello, Mrs. Houchin. I'm so pleased you brought Ashley to see me. You have the loveliest and kindest daughter in the world, so you must be pretty special yourself."

Iola could not see the mighty red blush lighting up Mrs. Houchin's face. "Thank you, Mrs. Taylor, for sharing your time and stories with Ashley," she said. "And, my goodness, for giving Ashley your home."

"It's been such a joy knowing Ashley. Perhaps she has already told you that I also have given her some special powers."

"Powers? What powers, Ashley?" her mother asked.

"Iola, I told my parents about the ring and the magic powers, but I don't think they believed me," Ashley said.

"Those powers?" her mother questioned, a pained expression on her face as she recalled Ashley's attempts to convince her and her husband that she rescued little people and talked to dolls.

"You know Ashley," Iola said, "I think from now on they just might take you a little more seriously. You have to be patient with them. Magic is something most grownups just don't understand." Iola paused for a moment to catch her breath. Mrs. Houchin stood wide-eyed by Ashley, unable to speak.

Iola continued, "I suppose you wondered why I left so suddenly and took away the dolls as well."

"Yes. Yes. I can't wait to find out," Ashley said.

"Well, Ashley, I could tell that this old body was wearing out pretty fast. It was hard for me to see anything, and walking took a big effort. All of my kin have passed on. I don't have anyone around to give my things to, so I sort of adopted you to be my family. Rather than scare you to death some day finding me incapacitated or even dead in my house, I decided to stage my exit while I still had some friends who would help out. I gave all of my dolls, except Julie, to Betsy from the Crosslines Christmas Store for needy children. She will see to it that all of the dolls will be given to little girls and boys at Christmas. Think about that!" she said with more emphasis. "Julie knows all of the stories those dolls have already told me, and at Christmastime this year they will go out and load up on some more. Julie will tell you everything she knows, and then it won't be too long and you will be blessed with an overflow of new doll stories."

Mrs. Houchin's expression had not changed for several minutes. She stood there astonished.

"Now you can do anything you want to with that house, Mrs. Houchin, but just remember, whoever lives there is going to have 180 dolls arriving on their front porch, one at a time, for many years to come. I was kind of hoping that Ashley would be there to receive them."

"I'll be there, Iola. I'll be there," Ashley replied.

Mrs. Houchin nodded meekly.

Iola continued, "I moved out here because all of my needs are taken care of. I wanted to wait until I got completely settled before I called for you, Ashley. I have met some wonderful new human friends who have many, many stories to tell. Perhaps you saw some of them when you walked in."

"Yes, I did, Iola. Seeing them as we walked in reminded me of the first day I met you in your parlor, with only candlelight and flashes of lightning to see by. I had that same feeling today when I walked passed those people in the glow of the setting sun."

"Good, Ashley, good. You see, they are my dolls now, and I would like for you to listen to their stories and pass them on. For example, Mrs. Burg lived much of her life in Eastern Europe, and she had to escape during the war, just like the Dubois family had to get away from Ada Kohln. Mrs. Hite was a famous ballerina in New York and danced in all of the great halls of Europe and America. Mr. Thiessen was a major-league baseball announcer, knew all of the great players and is full of sports tales. Mrs. Nelson raised three children on a small farm in South Dakota, taught school and ran races up Pikes Peak until she was 70 years old. Yes, every one of them has had an interesting life, and it would be such a shame to let their stories pass unheard."

Iola paused and took a long, deep breath. "Oh my. I'm so tired," she said weakly.

Mrs. Houchin had regained her composure enough to sense that Iola needed to rest.

"We've got to go, Ashley," she said in a barely audible voice.

Ashley moved closer to the bed and bent over so that her face was next to Iola's.

"I love you, Iola. I love you. I'll be back," Ashley said as she kissed Iola on the cheek. A lump began to grow in her throat, and tears welled up in her eyes.

As Ashley stroked Iola's left arm, the Dollmaker's

eyes closed and a smile struggled to enliven her face.

Ashley and her mother walked slowly out of the room, waving as they left. Although she could not see them, Iola waved back. The hallway was empty, as the residents were having dessert in the dining room. Ashley was oblivious to the loud chattering and bursts of laughter coming from the dining room as she sauntered to the exit. She was wondering if she would ever get to speak to Iola again.

Ashley and her mother drove home in total silence, each pondering with different understandings the momentous events of the last few months.

In the days that followed, Ashley found it much easier to fill her eager and wide-eyed parents in on every detail of her exciting adventures with the Mooncorn People and Iola Taylor. After much discussion, they agreed to keep this wonderful saga a secret in order to protect the power of Ashley's magic ring.

On January 3rd, they joined in Iola's 106th birthday celebration, their second of many trips to visit the beloved Dollmaker.

And magic seems to linger for all time in that enchanted hallway where, on weekend afternoons as the luminous sun is setting, Ashley or one of her friends sits in spellbound conversation with a fascinating doll of the Country Court.

Acknowledgments

◦◦◦

My family and our friends and acquaintances have provided nearly all of the material for *Ashley and the Dollmaker* and *Ashley and the Mooncorn People*, which preceded it. Ashley, our first-born grandchild, was the inspiration for both stories. I have been reminded more than once that with nine other grandchildren, I have a lot of work ahead. I am especially grateful to my mother, Ista Iola Taylor Grantham, a remarkably gifted woman who made and dressed dozens of porcelain dolls and gave them all away to family, friends and those in need. The motivation of the Dollmaker in this story to create dolls of "store-bought" quality for needy girls replays my mother's reaction to a real Christmas disappointment while growing up poor on an Oklahoma cotton farm. The story of Carol, the girl in the Dollmaker's first story, is based on events in the life of my wife, Carol Elaine Grantham, who has memories of real tornadoes in eastern Missouri. Twadie of the second story is in fact Santa's chief elf at the Crosslines Christmas Store, an organization in Kansas City, Kansas, that provides gifts for the needy. Keystone, Oklahoma, is currently under the water of Keystone Lake, in case anyone is inclined to investigate how those lottery dolls got switched. The swimming hole beneath the railroad tracks west of Pratt, Kansas, in story three still beckons, but the Mediocre Man Club never met again after its close call in the Wind Cave. And the Country Court represents one of hundreds of retirement centers across this nation, each filled with fascinating dolls just waiting for someone to listen to their stories.

My deepest thanks go to Craig Lueck for creating the cover, Jim Langford for designing the book layout, Deborah Lorenzi for critique and Lee Lueck for patient editing and creative input. Leathers Publishing pulled it all together to make the creation of this book an exceedingly pleasant task.

−JJG